I TRIED TO ~~~~~ HERS, NOT LOOK AT ~~~~~

She was trying to say something. I leaned forward.

"What?"

"You . . . took . . ."

Her voice trailed off.

I wrenched my eyes away from the spreading stain and leaned closer. Her eyes rolled away from me now, and she squirmed feebly, but the tension was going out of her face. It was turning pasty white, relaxed and soft.

She looked straight at me, seeming to be making an effort to hold on to consciousness.

"Do you know who did this to you, Rebecca?"

———————————— ★ ————————————

"Emma Chizzit is a sleuth to treasure and one of my favorites."

—Carolyn G. Hart

"Elderly women have long been favorite sleuths, but there has never been one quite like Emma Chizzit."

—Rave Reviews

"Emma Chizzit is a uniquely interesting power figure."

—Drood Review of Mystery

Forthcoming from Worldwide Mystery by
MARY BOWEN HALL

EMMA CHIZZIT AND THE SACRAMENTO STALKER

MARY BOWEN HALL

EMMA CHIZZIT
AND THE
QUEEN ANNE
KILLER

WORLDWIDE®

TORONTO • NEW YORK • LONDON
AMSTERDAM • PARIS • SYDNEY • HAMBURG
STOCKHOLM • ATHENS • TOKYO • MILAN
MADRID • WARSAW • BUDAPEST • AUCKLAND

EMMA CHIZZIT AND THE QUEEN ANNE KILLER

A Worldwide Mystery/March 1994

This edition is reprinted by arrangement with Walker
and Company.

ISBN 0-373-28014-9

EMMA CHIZZIT AND THE QUEEN ANNE KILLER

ONE

THE PLACE WAS an old Victorian, boarded up for years. No telling what I might find in there.

As soon as I'd gotten to the north side of Fairville, I'd spotted the house, a large Queen Anne with a handsome wraparound verandah. It nestled on a gentle slope, the Coast Range foothills rising behind, and overlooked a valley once filled with hayfields and fruit trees. Battalions of subdivisions marched toward it now, and an advance patrol of bulldozers and backhoes rooted in the remnants of a nearby apricot orchard—Damien Enterprises vehicles, sunlight gleaming on the signature stripes of crimson and pearl gray that marked everything Belle Damien put her hand to. The machinery chuffed and clattered, pulling out twisted old trees, digging trenches, and scraping the curved outlines of soon-to-be streets.

A ragged row of palm trees, grown perilously tall, lined the drive to the house. I drove into the front yard turnaround and brought my Dodge truck to a squeaking stop. A young woman stood beside a small car already parked there—a dressed-for-success type in a blue jacket and white bow-tie blouse. She was evidently a Damien minion, and she might give me problems. If I were a man, my age wouldn't matter, but people get edgy when they see a woman my age doing this kind of work—even a woman like me, broad-shouldered and tall.

"Hello," I hollered in my best gruff-but-competent voice. "I'm Emma Chizzit. A-1 Salvage."

"Roberta Moore," she said, "Damien Enterprises."

She gave me one of the those dubious looks I know all too well, taking in the truck's battered fenders, and, as I hopped out of the cab, my scuffed work boots and faded denim shirt.

I gave her no chance to balk. "Belle sent word you'd give me the key," I said, as if I were someone Belle sent word to every day. I moved quickly, striding over to her car and plucking the key to the house out of her hand. Then right away I made a show of climbing easily onto the back of my old pickup and hustling out tools.

It worked. She took off and left me alone.

I was disappointed when I got inside the Queen Anne. Some ignoramus had modernized it—replaced the old fixtures and doors with cheap stuff and put up a lot of Sheetrock and plywood. The place was a shambles, the floor strewn with the kind of leftover junk you find when careless tenants clear out and leave all their trash behind. I'd been told the original family had lived in the house until the sixties, but for years it had stood vacant. Now, courtesy of Belle Damien, it was to become the clubhouse for the Victorian Villa condo development.

I stood in the front hallway, looking around. Someone had been in here and had a fine old time. It didn't look like the work of homeless transients, more like vandals had worked the place over. Maybe kids, I thought, looking for amusement on days they didn't want to be in school.

The original staircase remained, the carved bannister making a graceful curve leading to the upstairs. I climbed up to have a look. The second floor hallway was undisturbed—everything neat and tidy, bedroom doors closed, and a trackless layer of dust on the floor. I checked a few of the rooms. There'd been less remodeling done up here, but there was no sign anything belonging to the original owners had been left in the rooms. A peace emblem had been spray-painted on one wall. In one closet was a hula hoop. I gave up on the idea of finding anything of value and went back downstairs. I'd decided to wrench the boards off a few windows, let the place air, and start on the outside.

Those upstairs rooms might still yield a few salable odds and ends, but if there was a treasure trove anywhere here, it was likely under the verandah. I loosened the paint-stuck ends of the lath sheating that surrounded the area below the porch, then got my flashlight to peer into the darker areas underneath. I'd had the right idea. The first thing I found was a bundle of carved oak pieces, sections of some small item of furniture that had been dismantled and packed flat. I hauled it out and spread the pieces in the side yard. It took me a few minutes to figure out that the sections, put together, made a pretty little cradle with a carved headboard.

I tied the pieces into a bundle again and stashed them in the cab of my truck, thinking I'd probably have time on my way home to stop by and see Joe Simpson. I knew he could make the cradle look like a million bucks. Well, I wasn't going to make a fortune from this, but there might be enough to pay for a river trip or some other nice outing.

I pulled out more stuff from under the porch: battered window screens, rolls of leftover linoleum, and the like. Then I stopped for a breather, wanting to give my back a chance to straighten out. The day was turning out to be even hotter than I'd expected. I'd agreed to do this job in spite of the midsummer heat and the hour's drive from Sacramento. My friend Frannie Edmundson knows Belle Damien and had gone out of her way to get me the work.

I need the occasional side job. I've got a place to live, thanks to Frannie, plus a little Social Security money, but I'm not one to sit home, trying to eke out an existence. So I got into the business of contracting to empty out old houses. I'm paid for hauling off the trash, and can sell anything of value that turns up. I've been in the business for a lot of years—cleaned out some funky places, too.

When a job comes along, I take it. I can't afford to be dainty. If I let a little hot weather stop me, I wouldn't make a dime all summer.

As I'd approached Fairville this morning the blast-furnace wind had started to die down, but not enough to let in any cool breezes from San Francisco Bay. I hadn't seen any trace of the summer fog that usually lapped over the hills to the west. Instead, the familiar ridges of the Coast Range stood out clearly, golden dry and dotted with scrub oak.

The garden of the old house, what was left of it, was as dry as the hills. The slope beside the verandah was nearly barren, an expanse of weed-splotched dirt, dry and cracked. One ragged row of pink amaryllis still bloomed alongside the privet hedge that marched unevenly down toward a picket fence at the bottom of the yard. I was admiring the spot of color afforded by the amaryllis, when I thought I saw a flurry of motion on the other side of the hedge.

I turned around and took a good look, even strolled part way down the slope, but couldn't see anyone. I don't mind working alone in odd places, but I'm no dummy when it comes to taking precautions. I went over to the truck and brought back my favorite insurance policy, a lightweight ax handle. It's as good a weapon as a baseball bat, and just my size. I figured to keep it close at hand while I finished cleaning underneath the verandah.

I went back to work, hauling out useless pieces of this and that. Then, back in the far recesses, I found a stack of doors. They looked to be interior doors that had been taken out when the place was remodeled—Grade A stuff, still with the original hardware, and certain to bring a good price at one of my favorite buyers, Demolition Engineers in West Sacramento.

As I was pulling out the last of the doors, I noticed a piece of cloth coming with it, caught on a hinge. I picked up my flashlight, knelt to get a better look, and saw a cloth-wrapped bundle stuffed in a shallow hole. The piece of cloth had been pulled from it—cotton flannel, it looked like in the flashlight beam, tattered and stained.

At first I didn't see what was sticking out at the edge of the bundle—a tiny hand, brownish and shriveled. Dear Lord! I pulled back, closed my eyes, and tried to tell myself I hadn't seen what I knew I'd seen.

I made myself look again, reach over, take the bundle, peel back the blanket. There it was, the mummified corpse of an infant. So tiny... dried... brown... almost like some kind of voodoo doll. The body was shrunken, but perfect in every detail. I studied the little face, the eyes squinched shut and the cheeks pulled tight. The baby's mouth was drawn back, the planes of its face taut. The expression was familiar to me, yet so out of place. My own little ones had sometimes looked like that when they were infants, hungry and getting ready to cry for a feeding.

I put the blanket back over the baby; careful to cover the tiny arm that stuck out, and rocked back on my heels, trying to collect myself.

I had an impulse to put the child back; no one would be the wiser. Some teenaged mother might have left it here, someone who knew she couldn't take care of her child. Or maybe when the baby was born, things weren't right. No, the baby had lived for a while. I'd seen a belly button, all healed, hadn't I? Good grief! I hadn't even noticed if the baby was a boy or a girl.

I reached again and unwrapped the blanket. The baby was a girl. I studied her for a moment, wondering how she'd died. Then I saw it.

A wire was pulled tightly around her neck.

TWO

I HAD TO REPORT what I'd found.

When I'd arrived that morning, I'd seen a pay phone outside a dilapidated cafe where I'd turned to come up the narrow road leading to the house. I hustled into my truck and went back to the intersection, checking the street sign so I could make sure to give the police good directions. Honolulu Road. Of all the names for a country lane leading to a nineteenth-century house, this was about the unlikeliest. I wondered what Belle Damien planned to do about a name so mismatched to her Victorian Villa concept. She'd get it changed, most likely—where there's money, there's always a way.

While I was on the phone with the police, I noticed that I could see the house clearly, as well as the driveway with its old palms and the side yard where I'd been working. Anyone watching from here could have seen me up there. Maybe someone had a chuckle at my expense when I'd gotten spooked and armed myself with the ax handle. No matter—a fortunate circumstance, actually. Maybe someone in the old cafe would know something about who had come and gone at the old place.

After I finished my call to the police, I decided I'd better call Belle Damien's office, too.

The rest of the day was a mess.

The police came right away and started stringing plastic tape around, marking the crime scene the way it's done on television. Then a vehicle from the coroner's office came, lights flashing. I was told I couldn't go home, but would have to wait for a police detective named Riley to show up.

The young woman from Damien Enterprises who'd given me the key to the house appeared about then, looking scared and uncertain. After a while, Riley showed up. He was a man nearly my age, who looked grumpy and sounded indifferent. He asked all the predictable questions and wrote down my answers without once looking me in the eye. I watched two burly men put the baby in some kind of miniature body bag, which they loaded onto a stretcher big enough for a football player. While this was going on, *La Belle Damien* herself arrived in a big Cadillac with a driver.

What on earth was *she* doing here?

Belle listened intently to what her assistant told her, all the while glancing in my direction, her long pearl pink nails drumming on a briefcase she never opened, and her face permanently adjusted to a noncommittal expression. I stared back, openly curious.

Belle, elegantly lean, wore a linen suit the color of silver with a matching silk blouse, and turquoise jewelry that obviously wasn't run-of-the-mill stuff. Her hair, also silvery gray, was done up in one of those nonchalantly perfect French twists. I had to give her credit. She was definitely a class act.

My friend Frannie had told me a lot about Belle. She's the widow of P.J. Damien—his second wife. She'd married the old tycoon long after he'd made a pile of money in the real estate boom after World War II. Even when he was alive—he'd died sometime around 1970—Belle had pretty much taken over the business.

Frannie felt sorry for Belle. Frannie said old P.J. had fooled around with a series of young girlfriends in those last years before he died. Belle had behaved magnificently, according to Frannie, always gracious and dignified, always diligent in keeping the Damien private lives as private as possible.

"People criticize Belle for being secretive," Frannie had said. "No one gives her credit for being a real lady."

Of course, Frannie had it all on hearsay. She didn't know Belle back in those days, Belle being one of her newer connections. But the truth seemed to be that old P.J. had been a thorough-going playboy, while Belle had settled in at the reins of Damien Enterprises. Maybe she'd had to do a lot of work, but I didn't think Belle needed much sympathy. From what little I knew, it seemed to me Belle was the type who enjoyed the tycoon business. She was putting up shopping centers and housing developments at a pace that made old P.J. look like an amateur. I had to admire her for being good at it, too. Still, I don't much like developers, on principle.

By the time Riley finished questioning me, I was about done gawking at Belle and had begun to turn my attention to the conversations around me. I heard someone say there would be an autopsy, probably an inquest. Meanwhile, the police photographer was getting ready to take a picture of my stack of doors. I didn't think I could take the doors with me, but I asked one of the uniformed officers.

"Nothing leaves here today, lady."

I'd have to change my expectations about money, or at least about how soon I'd get any.

The police were still pawing through all the stuff from under the verandah, but they let me go. I didn't waste any time getting back on the freeway and heading for home.

There was a battered old Karmann Ghia behind me on the freeway, traveling at about the same rate of speed. You notice a car like that; there aren't many Karmann Ghias on the road anymore. This one was an unusual color—faded orange, I guess, but darker, more toward dusty pumpkin. Miles went by and it was still there. I sped up. I slowed down. The car stayed a certain distance behind.

For a while I thought it was coincidence, but by the time we were approaching Sacramento, I was tired of the cat-and-mouse game. There was no sense being outright stupid—why should I lead whoever it was right into my front yard? When we got to West Sacramento, I took the Harbor Boulevard off-ramp; at the first intersection, I turned again and went into a restaurant parking lot. The Karmann Ghia made all the same turns, and when I pulled into the parking lot, it stopped nearby at the far side of an adjoining gas station. I was beginning to feel like a character in a spy story, except that the script was a little out of whack. A

Karmann Ghia, faded and battered, doesn't have the right aura. No *menace.*

I got out of my truck and walked to the restaurant, stopping outside to pretend to read the headlines of newspapers in the vending racks. Maybe, I thought wildly, the driver of the Karmann Ghia would get out and pretend to make a phone call from the booth on the gas station lot. So far, I hadn't been able to get a look at whoever it was. When I'd gotten out of my truck, I'd managed only to see the huddled outline of somebody ducked down in the driver's seat.

I went on into the restaurant and stood just inside the door, waiting. Maybe I was safer inside. It seemed to me I waited inside that restaurant forever, but I guess it was only a few minutes. When I came back out, I saw a woman moving cautiously toward my truck. She was drab and pathetic-looking, decidedly less menacing than the Karmann Ghia.

"Hey!" I yelled.

She jerked around, then froze and stood staring at me like a startled jackrabbit. When I yelled again and started to run toward her, she fled. In an instant she was in the Karmann Ghia, gunning the engine. She must have left the keys in the ignition. Before I could get to my truck, her car lurched out of the lot.

THREE

I'D HAD ENOUGH for one day—too much. I started up the truck and headed home.

As I crossed the bridge into Sacramento, I searched the horizon for sight of the tall shade trees that mark the area where I live. It's an older neighborhood, close to downtown, an island of better-class homes and tranquility. I was eager for a cool shower and the solace of my quiet, tree-shaded apartment.

My friend Frannie is also my landlady. She and her husband—once a member of the state legislature—had chosen their home well. Frannie's been a widow for a long time now, but she's never moved to smaller quarters, which turned into a boon for me.

Frannie's a friend from my high school days, and when she heard I was down on my luck some years ago, she insisted I come to live in the old chauffeur's apartment above her garage. The arrangement has worked out well. I have a nice home, and in return I'm a jack-of-all-trades for things Frannie needs done—something of a gardener, too, since I take care of anything her lawn-mowing man doesn't.

I pulled into the driveway and put my truck in the garage, keeping a wary eye out for Frannie. She's a loyal friend, but I didn't want to have to deal with her right now. I was glad, as always, to see my cat, Sourpuss, waiting on the little porch at the top of the stairs. He followed me inside, yowling in his gritty old voice, serving notice that I'd been gone far too long, and he was hungry.

"Hold on, old boy."

In the bedroom, the message light was blinking on the answering machine Frannie had insisted on buying for me. Of course, it was Frannie's voice on the tape.

"Emma, I just wanted to tell you not to make plans for Sunday afternoon. We've got to go to Clara's art show. Remember? I told you Clara might have her art on display, when Belle opens her new shopping center."

At least she didn't want to see me tonight—but there went Sunday. For the umpteenth time I wished Frannie would decide she was brave enough to drive her car in fast traffic instead of roping me into doing her freeway driving. Or that I didn't feel I owed it to her.

"I promised Clara we'd come, so I wanted you to know right away. If it's not too late, call me when you get in, will you, Emma?"

It was too early to get out of calling Frannie. I'd have to tell her about finding the baby, and go through the whole mess again. But Frannie could wait until I'd given Sourpuss his supper. Himself was already positioned by his food dish, unblinking yellow eyes fixed on me—his best feed-me stare.

The phone rang just as I was opening the refrigerator.

"Emma?" Frannie again. "I just heard about it from Clara—I mean the dead baby—and I saw you come home."

Good grief! How did she always manage to find out everything so fast? I tucked the phone to my ear, trailing the long cord as I moved from the bedroom back to the kitchen. I heard the whole story of what had happened at the old house, as explained to Frannie by Clara, who'd called to check on the details of the art exhibit, and gotten it from someone in Belle Damien's office. I listened and um-hummed.

"Gracious!" Frannie concluded. "You must be all done in."

I agreed, at the same time knowing what was coming next.

"I've just fixed a lovely pasta salad for us, with some of that scrumptious dry salami from the Downtown Deli. When I thought of you sitting up there all alone, after—"

"Frannie, I am awfully tired."

"That's exactly why, Emma, you never cook properly for yourself."

Frannie has two responses to stressful situations. She goes shopping, and she prepares enormous quantities of food. Both responses had come into play this time; there'd be no getting out of the invitation.

"They had some lovely Persian melons at the market. I've got raspberry sherbet, too."

"Thank you, Frannie," I said, mustering as much enthusiasm as I could. "I'll be down in a few minutes."

Frannie had set up our supper in a little room toward the back of the house from the *porte cochere,* the kind of room that used to be called a sun porch. Frannie had had a decorator in and got it all done up in white wicker furniture and potted ferns, and now she called it the patio room. Normally we'd sit down to a meal in her breakfast nook, but Frannie had designated this a semi-special occasion. She was hostessing with a flair, wheeling in our meal on a serving cart. As much as I wanted to be alone to sort out my thoughts, I'd have to sit through the entire event.

Frannie's plump body was encased in a long floral-print shift, her hair pulled up and done in glossy brown curls. Her cooking, as always, had produced a delicious meal. I did my best to appreciate it, despite Frannie's barrage of questions. Her sympathy for my feelings was genuine, but Frannie never could resist the urge to speculate about the gossipy aspects of any situation.

"I found out that the house was part of the old Jorgensen ranch," she told me. "The Jorgensens were once one of the most prominent families in Solano County. You don't suppose that anyone in the Jorgensen family..."

"Frannie, I don't suppose anything."

"Oh. You're probably right. It couldn't have been any of the Jorgensens—fine people like that, they just couldn't have. But then they fell on hard times, you know, had to rent the house out to such trashy people."

I began to wonder if the woman in the Karmann Ghia had once lived in the house. She would certainly match Frannie's idea of "trashy people."

"It must have been one of those tenants. Are you listening to me, Emma?"

"Yes. I was just thinking about who might have lived there."

"Well! Belle said she got rid of those tenants right away."

"You talked to Belle?"

"Of course. I kept calling until I could catch her at home. I didn't want her to think that I . . . that we . . . would think that she . . ."

"Good grief! Why on earth would we think Belle had anything to do with it?"

"Well, people talk, you know. And Belle's so sensitive about gossip. When we go to Clara's art show, I don't want you to . . ."

"For God's sake, Frannie!"

She looked hurt. To change the subject, I asked what Clara had been doing lately, which set Frannie rattling along with great enthusiasm.

A few years back Clara had been pretty rebellious—not that I blamed her. Her mother, Melissa Edmundson, Frannie's sister-in-law, is one of the world's foremost controlling mothers. She hadn't wanted a daughter, but a marionette on strings. Poor little Clara had to look pretty all the time, smile sweetly, and be nice to all the friends her mother chose for her. Small wonder she'd made a declaration of independence when she'd gotten to high school, mixing herself up with kids her mother was sure to disapprove of—the orange hair and black eyelids set.

Melissa and Frannie had been beside themselves. I'd been worried, too. But lately Frannie had been bragging to the skies about Clara. She'd gone away to college and majored in art. Nowadays she was involved with her art work, and beginning to find ways to get paid for it.

Frannie was still going on.

"... of course, Melissa's none too happy about *that*."

I'd missed something. No matter. I was sure to hear about it sooner or later. Probably sooner. I had my own concerns to worry about.

As a matter of fact, I spent half the night worrying. I had a long discussion with myself over whether to report to the Fairville police that I'd been followed by the woman in the Karmann Ghia. The only link to the discovery of the dead baby was that both events had occurred the same day. Of course, the woman in the Karmann Ghia may have been spying on me earlier in the afternoon. For the most part it seemed to me that the death of the baby was one of those tragic events for which no explanation is ever found, and being followed like that might be just another one of life's inexplicable events.

But I'm not much on *inexplicable* as an explanation—especially when people start following me around.

I decided that on Sunday, after I'd taken Frannie to the shopping center party, I'd drive over in her Mercedes and scout around in the vicinity of the old house, to see if I could spot the Karmann Ghia. I could ask some questions at that cafe, too. I'd be wearing my dress-up outfit, so there wasn't much chance anyone would suspect I was the same person who'd come around in work clothes and an old truck.

My truck. The antique cradle I'd found under the verandah was still stashed in it.

FOUR

THE NEXT DAY I phoned to report that I had the cradle.

"Fairville police." A woman's voice.

"Good morning." I cleared my throat. "I'd like to talk to Mr. Riley. I guess it's Detective Riley."

"Mr. Riley isn't in. May I take a message?"

"My name is Emma Chizzit. I'm the one who... Well, yesterday I . . ."

"Yes." There was sympathy in her voice. "You found the baby."

I was relieved not to have to explain.

"I'm sorry," she said, "but you probably won't be able to talk with Mr. Riley. Today is his last day on the job. He's retiring. As a matter of fact, he's over at the city hall right now, signing papers in the personnel office. And after that he's going directly to the retirement lunch."

"I forgot to mention something to him yesterday. Is there someone else taking over the case that I can talk to?"

"Not right now. Almost everyone is over getting ready for the lunch. But would you like to leave a message for Mr. Holmes? He's the new man, he'll be taking over the case.''

"Yes. I took something from under the porch yesterday. I'd already put it in my truck, and forgot about it.''

"Mr. Holmes doesn't officially start until Monday, but if you think it's important...."

"No," I said quickly. "Just tell the new man I'll check in with him on Monday.''

I'd decided to report about being followed, but that could wait, too.

I prowled around my apartment, restless at having no plans now that I wasn't going to be taking the cradle over to Fairville. I put on a pot of coffee, sat down to wait for it to brew, and pulled Sourpuss onto my lap.

"I suppose I could have left a more complete message," I told him, as I worked my fingers along his chin. "Maybe there is a connection... baby and cradle. Or some clue about who the baby was. But the cradle was under one end of the porch, the baby at the other, so it's not as if this would be crucial evidence, with fingerprints on it or something."

Sourpuss settled down, purring loudly.

"It's not as if I'd noticed anything about the cradle that might yield some useful information.

Besides, the cradle must have been there for years—the baby certainly was—a few more days isn't going to make any difference.''

"Yeow," Sourpuss said. I'd stopped petting him.

"Okay, Mr. Conscience. I'll confess. I want to show the cradle to Joe and get an idea about how much it'll be worth. *Now* are you satisfied?''

The cat's yellow eyes stared up at me.

"Oh, come on, Sourpuss. The woman in the Karmann Ghia? Whatever she wanted, I'll bet you ten sardines we don't have to worry about it.''

LATER THAT AFTERNOON, when I figured he'd be through work, I headed over to see Joe Simpson. Joe and I have a good arrangement. He's a wizard at turning junk into antiques, and he's willing to wait for his money until the item's been sold. He works and lives on his boat, at a yacht club marina on River Road, down toward the delta from Sacramento.

I drove along the levee, enjoying the cool westerly breeze that had at last begun to come in from San Francisco. I turned in at the yacht club, circled through the parking lot, and at the far end jounced onto the bumpy track to Joe's mooring place. At the end of the road, I took the cradle out of the truck and started down the path.

Every time I visit Joe I take time to savor the smell of river weeds and damp silt and listen to the gentle sloosh of the river lapping against the shore. When I get farther down the path, I know I'll hear the soft wail of Joe's harmonica. Joe always has his bottle of beer and a good session with the harmonica at the end of the day.

He looked up when I stepped onto his little makeshift dock.

"Evening, Emma."

Joe has a gentle Oklahoma accent. He's a pleasant, easygoing sort, the kind you never notice in a crowd. His eyes are his one striking feature—blue and intense. The kind you can just about fall into and get lost in. But I've never let myself get that kind of close with Joe, having never wanted to chance wrecking a good friendship.

I told Joe the whole works—finding the cradle and then the baby, and the strange business about being followed. Then I showed him the cradle pieces.

While Joe studied them, I thumbed through his beat-up catalogue of antiques. It had pictures of items that had been sold at auction, and the prices each had brought. I had to go back and forth through the pages, not having a name for the style of the cradle. But I could find nothing, no clue about a possible price. There wasn't a thing in the catalogue like it.

I gave up and watched Joe. He'd run his hands thoughtfully over the carved headboard, then begun inspecting the way the notched side pieces fit together.

"What do you think?" I asked.

"Good quality wood, nice workmanship.... Somebody carved this by hand."

I reached over for the headboard, wanting to have a closer look at the carving. At first it had just seemed like some kind of fancy scrollwork, but now I saw something else—the initials *AD*. The *D* was the right half of a design made in a circle, and the *A* was snuggled up to it to make the left half.

"Look, it's got initials," I said to Joe. At the same time my mind pounced on the idea that the *D* could stand for Damien.

Joe took the headboard and turned it so the light hit the carving from the side.

"Yep. *AD*."

He ran his fingertips over the carving.

"Really nice.... Look how perfect the round is on these letters."

"These initials—they could mean there's a link to the Damien family."

"How's that?"

"Damien Enterprises owned the old house, owned it for years, and—no, it's just too darned pat."

Joe nodded.

"Probably is."

He picked up his harmonica.

"It was strange," I went on, "that Belle showed up at the house. Why would she do a thing like that?"

Joe shrugged and blew a few random notes on the harmonica.

"And you know something else? Frannie's talked a lot about how secretive Belle is about the Damien family."

Joe fixed his blue eyes on me, sending his eyebrows up in that quizzical way of his.

"Well, what she said was that Belle was very sensitive to gossip, because there'd been so much talk about the Damien family."

"How so? What kind of talk?"

"For one thing, there was a big age difference between Belle and old P.J. It's a good guess she married him for his money, or at least for more money than she already had. Also, from what

Frannie knows, the one who really got a big boost up by marrying for money was P.J. himself—the first time around.''

Joe chuckled, and allowed that was one way to get a good start in real estate. Then he took up his harmonica again and started in on ''Red River Valley.'' I sat contentedly for a while, watching the river and the sunset, sniffing the breezes, and studying pink sky reflections in the slow-moving river.

"You still saving for a canoe trip?'' Joe asked after he'd finished the song.

I said I was, and that maybe, after I'd gotten the doors and the cradle back and sold them, I'd have enough. But my mind was on those initials. Tomorrow was Saturday, but there was bound to be someone on duty at the Fairville Police Department, maybe even Mr. Whatever-his-first-name-was Holmes. If the things I knew got put together with the things the police had been able to find out, maybe I wouldn't be so plagued with all this *inexplicable* stuff.

I'd go back to the plan I'd had this morning— take the cradle over to Fairville first thing.

FIVE

As I DROVE TO FAIRVILLE the next morning, I made up my mind to try talking with Holmes first—if he was on the job yet—but I'd give equal priority to trying to get those doors. I felt nettled about giving up, for now, my money for anything I'd found at the house, and there was no telling how long I'd have to wait before I could finish the job and collect my pay for the contract.

My doors. I repeated the phrase to myself as I approached the collection of temporary buildings behind a shopping center that now housed the Fairville Police Department. Fairville has grown drastically in recent years. The police department had been relocated to the west edge of town, but I'd only found that out after I'd circled the city hall three times before finding a parking place.

Behind the police station counter was a young woman in a police blue polyester uniform; her name badge identified her as D. Hughes. When she offered to help me, I recognized her voice. She was the one I'd spoken to on the phone.

"I'm Emma Chizzit," I said.

"Oh, yes." She pushed back wearily at her dishwater blonde hair. Her gaze was steady and confident—hazel eyes, with an honest look.

I asked whether Holmes was available.

"He's been in and out," she said, "sort of getting a head start on the job. But he's not here right now, and I don't know if he'll be back again today or not."

"There was something about the case I thought he might want to know."

"Can *I* help you?"

I was thinking about that, wondering how to explain everything in a succinct message, when a telephone on the desk buzzed.

"Excuse me," she said, and tended to the phone call. Then she asked again if she could help me.

By this time I'd decided to just ask about my doors. She seemed busy. No need to bother her when Holmes probably wouldn't get the message today anyhow.

When I asked about the doors, she told me she thought the inventorying of the items under the porch had been finished.

"I think all the samples that were brought in were sent over to the lab," she added, "but I don't know if the paperwork is finished."

No paperwork, no doors, I thought. And no money.

"I'm sorry," she said.

Just then a heavy hand landed on my shoulder.

"Aren't you the one who found the dead baby?"

I turned around, startled. The hand belonged to a balding, moist-faced giant of a man, a fellow with a huge torso and short legs, also wearing police blue polyester.

"You discovered that baby, right?" He beamed at me. "Been wanting to meet you. You must be *some* lady." He took his sweaty paw away from my shoulder to offer a handshake. "I was off duty that day, real sorry to miss out on it. Been on the force thirty years, name's Vince Valenti. Yes, sir! Sorry to have missed it."

"I'm Emma Chizzit."

He grabbed my hand with one paw, putting the other on top to make sure I wasn't going to get my hand away.

"Emma, you just call me Vince. Vince Valenti, don't you forget it." He winked at me. "Say, that must have been a real surprise. I mean, you're going along doing your job, and then—whappo!—you're looking at—" He was patting my hand now, still not letting go. "Oh, Jeez, I'm sorry. Maybe you don't want to talk about it."

He apparently had his own interpretation of the pained look on my face. "I don't," I said, still wondering how to retrieve my hand. "I just came back to—"

"Yeah, you want to get some doors out of there. I heard. Don't you worry about a thing. Old Vince here is gonna take care of you."

He gave my hand one final squeeze, then hurried around behind the counter.

"Debbie," he said, pawing through the papers on a desk at the back of the room. "Be a sweetheart and help me find that stuff."

"Mr. Valenti," she began, "you know what—"

"Aw, come on, Debbie. Anybody starts to give you a bad time, you just tell them that old Vince..." He pounced on a file folder. "Aha! Found it!"

He took the file and made a big show of tucking it under his arm. Debbie stood up, but he grabbed her by the shoulder and gently made her sit down again.

"Hold off, Debbie. You won't get in trouble. You just tell 'em I took this and lit out when you weren't looking." He winked broadly at me. "Come on, Emma."

Debbie and I exchanged glances. She shrugged. What happened with the stuff from under the verandah couldn't really be all that important, I thought. Not if the laboratory work was already taken care of.

Vince put one of his huge arms across my shoulders and walked me out the door, keeping up a steady stream of gab. He'd been around there longer than anyone else, he said, so they weren't going to tell him what to do. He was retiring this winter, had to. So, they didn't like this, they could fire him—right? And, he said, he'd take his own car to go over to the old house with me.

Vince's car was a big dusty old Chevy—by my guess a decommissioned police car. He drove ahead of me to Honolulu Lane, gesturing at every turn as if I might get lost if he didn't. Once we were there, Vince insisted on loading the doors onto the back of my truck for me, all the while talking a mile a minute.

"Emma, like I said before, you must be *some* lady. You do this kind of work all by yourself? Kinda dangerous work for a woman, seems to me. You ought to have a man around to protect you. Like a partner."

I kept quiet, but Vince must have been used to people not answering him.

"You live over in Sacramento, right? Too bad you don't live around here. I could help you maybe with heavy stuff when you got a job to do. Look at this." He picked up a door in each huge hand, holding his arms out straight. "See, still strong as an ox. I work out, you know, lift weights. Used to play football." He set the two doors in the truck, then stood gazing dreamily into space. "Yep, back at Redwood Junior College." He sighed. "Good old R.J.C. You should have seen us, fall of '46."

He turned to me, enthusiasm shining in his eyes.

"You like football? Bet you know about R.J.C. It's over in Santa Rosa—a farm team for Cal, always has been. They even call the team the Bear Cubs. Those were great days. Yessir, we had a great team in '46. You live around here then? Bet you heard about us, huh?"

"More or less," I said.

"Right! R.J.C. was known for football—that and for being a party school. The guys used to try for what they called a gentleman's grade point average—a perfect C straight across the board. They used to joke about it. No joke to me, though, I worked to keep my grades up. Didn't want to get kicked off the team. Say, you ever go to football games?"

"There's only one door left," I said. "We're just about through now."

"Oh. Yeah."

He loaded the last door onto the back of the truck, then used a forearm to wipe his brow. He tucked in his shirt and ran his hands through the remnants of his thinning hair.

"You sure you don't want nothing but the doors today?" His eyes were on mine, intent and eager. "Hey—I bet you're curious about the case. You want to know anything about it? I read all the reports."

"Oh?"

"Weird case. They're trying to figure out when the baby got put there. It was after the place was remodeled, though."

"How do they know that?"

"The doors were there first. Somebody dug in alongside them, sorta made a tunnel to the little hole they put the baby in."

Vince turned toward the verandah, grabbing me by the arm.

"Come on, I'll show you."

"That's all right, I don't need to see...."

But he had me firmly in tow. Then he stopped.

"Oh-oh. You see that?"

He jerked his thumb toward the slope below the rear of the house. A Damien Enterprises pickup was parked there. The truck stood empty, the door on the driver's side hanging open.

"Emma," Vince said, his voice taking on urgent tones. "I been saying a gal like you needs someone around. That don't seem suspicious—but what if you was working here all by yourself? I'm gonna check out that vehicle."

Vince went over to make a big thing out of inspecting the truck, which didn't make much sense to me. It was empty, obviously—but where was the driver?

I strolled toward the back of the house, then down along the far side of the privet hedge where I'd glimpsed a flurry of movement the day I found the baby. Sure enough, there was a shallow ditch running along here—but no one hiding in it. I moved up the slope, strolling toward the house. There was no one skulking here, either.

"Nothing," Vince said, coming back from his inspection of the pickup. "Keys in the ignition, no one near. Can't be too careful, you know."

I edged back toward my truck, wary that he might drape an arm around my shoulders again.

"Probably just someone working in that field," Vince said. "But it's funny they parked here."

"Thanks, Vince," I said, "for helping me. And for taking time out like this."

"Great. Sure. No problem. What they going to do, fire me?" He laughed a ha-ha to say he didn't take this idea seriously. "Say, you got time for a cup of coffee?"

"No, thanks. I've got to go."

I'd managed by this time to escape into the cab of my truck.

"Lunch, maybe," he said, lounging against the open truck window. "It's almost time for lunch. You got to eat lunch, anyways."

"I'm sorry, I've got to get going. I want to get back to Sacramento in time to sell these doors today."

"Yeah. Sure."

The poor jerk was lonely. I gave him my best smile, now that I was about to make good my escape. "Nice to have met you, Vince."

"You remember. You call me, anytime. You can count on old Vince. Anytime."

I started backing out of the driveway.

"Don't forget," he hollered after me. "Vince Valenti, at your service!"

I drove off slowly, watching in my rearview mirror for Vince's dusty old Chevy. He caught up and followed me for a while, until I began to think he intended to escort me all the way home. Good Lord! I didn't want that lonely fool camping on my doorstep, no matter how good-hearted he might be. Before long, he turned the other way, apparently headed for the police station, and I breathed a sigh of relief.

I turned back toward the old Queen Anne. I'd been sure at first that the Damien truck belonged to someone putting in overtime on the condo project. Now, I wasn't so sure, and I didn't want yet another item to be filed away under *inexplicable*. I saw no harm in going back for another look, even without Old Lonely for protection.

SIX

WHEN I GOT BACK to the Queen Anne, there was no sign of the Damien pickup, but I noticed that the front door of the house was slightly open. Had it been that way all the time Vince and I were loading my doors? Curiosity got the better of my common sense—but not before I'd fished my trusty ax handle out of the tool box. Clenching it firmly, and feeling a little foolish, I climbed the porch stairs, then stood just outside the door to listen.

Nothing.

I went on in—careful not to make a sound—and had a look around. The downstairs rooms were the same—junk strewn on the floor, closets and cupboards standing open. I checked upstairs. Someone had been here. Where I'd expected to see the dusty floor of the upstairs hall marked only by my own footprints, I saw old newspapers littered around the landing. Feeling a sudden sense of alarm, I stood motionless, ax handle at the ready, studying the scene and listening. After a moment I reached out with my foot, moving the nearest newspaper so I could see what was on the yellowed pages. It was a copy of the *Globe-Tattler*, one of those scandal sheets they sell at supermarkets. Nearby were pages from the *Fairville Reporter*. My attention was taken by a photo on a torn front page of the *Reporter*, showing a scene of the big civil rights march on Washington—1963, I thought. Then I noticed that one of the bedroom doors was open; I was certain I'd closed them all behind me. Inside I could see things that had been in the closet but were now strewn across the floor.

I retreated silently back down the stairs. Logic told me that whoever had been here had probably come and gone in the Damien pickup. Still, neither logic nor ax handle was enough to keep me from wanting to get out of the house as fast as possible.

The Fairville Police should be told about this. But I wasn't about to return to the station and chance another encounter with Vince, so when I got to the dilapidated cafe on the corner I parked by the pay phone—all the while keeping an eye on the house. Debbie answered the phone. Thanking my lucky stars it wasn't Vince, I told her what I'd discovered.

Then I skedaddled.

DRIVING BACK toward Sacramento, I gave some thought to whether the Damien pickup might really have been connected to the ransacking of the old house. The truck could easily have been left there by a construction worker whose errand took longer than he'd expected. For that matter, someone might have gotten in and gone through the things upstairs at any time since the day I'd found the baby.

When I'd come into the house that first time, I hadn't been surprised that the downstairs was trashed. The police must have been coming in and out of the place, and probably had checked upstairs, but whatever they'd found must have seemed quite predictable to them. Stuff was strewn all over downstairs, why not upstairs, too? Come to think of it, I'd probably been mistaken thinking that kid vandals had trashed the downstairs. Whoever had ransacked the upstairs had probably been working over the downstairs, too. Which meant that somebody was looking for something, even before I'd found the baby.

Either the ransacker was unconnected to the dead baby, or the entire situation was a lot more complicated than I'd thought. Meanwhile, I could take my choice: either I suspected someone driving a Damien pickup, or the mousey woman with the Karmann Ghia. Unless both were the same. Or I could work on the problem of why anyone would be rummaging through the Queen Anne, and whether he—or she—had found what they were looking for.

Tomorrow, after I'd delivered Frannie to the art show, I'd come back and ask a raft of questions at the old cafe. The folks there must have seen at least some of the goings-on at the old house.

I got to West Sacramento in time to take the doors over to the Demolition Engineers yard and sell them, then headed home for a cool shower and a chance to think things over. But as I turned the corner onto our street, I saw Melissa Edmundson's car pulling away, and as soon as I'd put my truck in the garage, Frannie hallooed at me from her back porch. She was bubbling with some kind of secret excitement, I could tell.

"Goodness! I've had the most exciting day. Melissa and I went to Belle's new shopping center to help Clara set up her exhibit. The place is just gorgeous."

Frannie launched into a description of the shopping center. I'd have been more interested in hearing about Clara's art show, but there was no point in trying to derail Frannie.

"Wait till you see it," she kept saying.

I reminded her that I would see it. The next day, in fact.

"Stay a minute longer," Frannie urged. "I'll fix us some iced tea."

Now what? Frannie's giggly enthusiasm had returned full force.

"So the shopping center looks fine, and Clara's art show is all set up," I said. "What else?"

Frannie waggled a finger at me.

"Emma, there's no keeping secrets from you."

"So..."

"I met a new friend. His name is Christian Whitaker."

I listened; Frannie enthused.

Christian Whitaker, it seemed, was a real estate consultant who'd stopped by to have a look at the new shopping center. He was handsome and dressed well. He'd been exceedingly helpful, had come over and spent a great deal of time helping set up Clara's watercolors. He knew about art; he knew about architecture.

"And such lovely manners!" Frannie stopped then, her mood switching abruptly. "I wish Clara would meet some young man just as nice. Instead, she's..."

"She's what?"

"She's involved with—well, Melissa's really upset about it. Clara should be looking to her future prospects, if you know what I mean, not going off on crusades. Instead, she's so involved in everything that Indian group wants."

Frannie's voice held a hint of disdain. An echo of what Melissa'd had to say, I was certain. Frannie's not the kind to be prejudiced.

"Well, what do they want?"

"I don't know. They're on some sort of crusade and need to raise money. They were setting up to sell their baskets right next to Clara's art exhibit."

"Do you know where the Indians are from?"

"Oh, that Madrone *rancheria* up north of Fairville somewhere. They're Pomo, I guess."

I was intrigued. Pomo baskets are some of the finest anywhere, and they don't go on the market all that often.

Frannie was going on again about the man she'd met when I glanced out the kitchen window. A red Datsun Z was pulling into the *porte cochere*. None of Frannie's friends, so far as I knew, were the kind to favor a muscle car like this, especially one with oversize tires. A man was getting out, looking around expectantly. He was handsome, the kind of looks you'd have to call leonine: a large head, a thick mane of wavy white hair, and a broad, furrowed face. He looked like he had just showered, and was dressed in a knit shirt and slacks—a short-necked and barrel-chested man, still surprisingly trim around the middle for someone his age.

I gestured toward the car.

"Who's that?"

Frannie peeked out, then jumped up, and began smoothing her hair.

"Oh, my!"

The girlish response meant only one thing. This was Christian Whitaker, the guy she'd met earlier today.

He looked around again, then reached back into his car, and took out a brown paper bag. Frannie, all atwitter by now, hurried to the door. I stood up, preparing to make a quick exit.

Whitaker's paper bag contained a bottle of champagne, which sent Frannie scurrying to get out her best silver ice bucket and tall champagne glasses—all the while protesting that I shouldn't leave yet. Whitaker was laying on the charm with a trowel, favoring both me and Frannie with hackneyed gallantries and a high-wattage smile.

He was handsome enough. The only way you could fault his appearance was that his nose seemed a little broad and flattened. It had the look of having been broken once. He could have been an athlete, or maybe in his salad days he was a brawler.

It wasn't his looks that went against him, as far as I was concerned. Every time he opened his mouth or cranked up that smile, I liked his tin-plated charm less. Frannie was really going for it, fluttering and putting a lot of lilt into her voice.

Whitaker shortly announced it was "time for some bubbly."

He opened the bottle, displaying considerable expertise, and poured champagne into three glasses.

"Here you are, my dears," he blandished, beaming equally at each of us. "No need to let lovely ladies go thirsty."

Frannie responded with a skilled bit of eyelash flapping.

"Thank you, kind sir."

Whitaker turned to me.

"And, fair one..."

I told him no thanks, I didn't drink. He looked discomfitted, but nonetheless hoisted his glass in a little toast to me.

"Here's to a lovely lady,"—in mid-speech he swung back toward Frannie—" and to you, lovely lady. This time his voice lingered over the *lovely*. He clinked his glass against Frannie's.

She was having a glorious time. But then she always did when men paid attention to her. Frannie loves to flirt, she'll do it the same way she glances in the mirror to see if she has her makeup on straight. Usually, after a man has paid attention to her for a while, Frannie is all through. I've seen her say good-bye so graciously, it would take some fool a half hour to comprehend he'd been given the gate.

I was most sincerely hoping that would be the scenario this time. Meanwhile, I thought, I'd better put on a minimum show of good manners.

"Frannie tells me you're a real estate consultant, Mr. Whitaker."

He leaned over and patted my arm.

"Call me Christian, please."

"Christian specializes in commercial development and shopping centers."

Whitaker was off and running with this, glibly comparing Belle's new shopping center with others in southern California and on the East Coast.

I didn't like the situation at all. Whitaker's real estate talk notwithstanding, I suspected his major endeavor was trolling for rich widows. Frannie might get tired of him, but first things would get sticky. She always got me embroiled in helping her when it came time to give one of these Lotharios his walking papers. Whitaker would be harder to get rid of than most. Once his type has gotten the scent of money, they don't give up easily.

At least I was off the hook for taking Frannie to Belle's party tomorrow. Whitaker would take her. It was a mixed blessing, because now I wouldn't have Frannie's Mercedes for protective cover when I went prowling around to see if I could spot the Karmann Ghia.

SEVEN

SUNDAY I WENT to the Fairville police station first thing, determined to get the cradle out of my truck and off my conscience. I walked in, lugging the bundle of cradle pieces. My bad luck, Vince was on Sunday duty.

"Aw, Emma," he said, mournful as a wounded puppy. "What you did yesterday—you should never have gone in that house without me."

I got a full sermon on all the reasons I needed his protection.

"Look, Vince," I said finally, "don't you think information about these initials on the cradle ought to go into a report somewhere?"

"Oh...yeah. Geez, I gotta write that down for Emerson Holmes. I wish I was handling the case. I'd remember something like that—wouldn't have to write it down."

"Debbie said he'd be taking over."

"Um-hum." Vince looked dejected. "Ordinary guys aren't good enough for them any more. They got to have some know-it-all with a fancy degree."

"I'm sure you could have handled it just fine," I said. No harm in making him feel a little better.

"Aw..." He beamed, embarrassed but delighted.

"Tell me about the new man."

"Fancy-pants!" Vince snorted. "He was in here this morning. Real smooth, in a suit and necktie—a white shirt, too. I could tell it was the kind you get done up at a laundry instead of washing at home."

He squared his shoulders, pursed his lips, and made a gesture as if he were straightening a necktie. Then he spoke in a mimicking tone. "'Just checking in. Good idea to hit the ground with my feet moving tomorrow.'" Vince snorted again. "Geez!"

"He'll probably settle down after a while," I suggested.

I was glad to learn about Holmes's credentials. Vince was a good and stalwart man, but a little spiffy professionalism around here seemed like a fine idea to me. I'd come in to see Holmes first thing tomorrow.

"Betcha Holmes will make a big deal about the initials on the cradle," Vince said. "Run a computer check or something."

"I wonder," I said, "if those initials match the name of anyone who used to live in that house."

"Gosh. I can't remember if there's anything in Riley's report, but I'll get it for you." He went into another room, then came back with a file folder. "Let's see.... Here it is. The statement from Belle Damien."

"What did she say?"

"Um ... she ... I'll read it to you. 'Mrs Damien stated that she and her late husband, P.J. Damien, bought the house in January 1964. It was then occupied by tenants, and was in the hands of a rental agent, C.B. Miller.' Hey, I know him."

"What else does it say?"

"Not much. The Damiens didn't like the tenants, had them evicted."

"Did she say why?"

"Naw. Just that they were undesirable. That's all there is here. 'Mrs. Damien claimed to know nothing about the tenants. They were undesirable, she had the agent evict them, and the house has since been unoccupied.'"

"Vince, you said you knew the rental agent."

"Sure. Clem Miller. He's been a real estate guy around here for a long time. He just retired last year."

"Maybe he remembers something about those tenants."

"I'll go see him. Soon's I find out something, I'll let you know."

"Thanks, Vince," I said, getting ready to leave.

"Your phone number's in the file," Vince said, trailing me to the door. "I'll call you right away."

Now I'd done it—let myself in for a phone call from Old Lonely. But maybe he would find out something.

Meanwhile, I figured there'd be no harm in doing a little sleuthing on my own, asking questions at the old cafe.

I FELT REASONABLY confident I wouldn't be recognized. I was dressed in a silk shirt and my best slacks; no one would be looking for the worker who'd been up at the Queen Anne to be coming around—and I could park the truck down the street out of sight.

The cafe looked deserted. I walked up to the porch and went on in, letting the screen door bang behind me to announce my presence. On my left were a few short aisles of convenience-store groceries, where a bald man with a handlebar mustache was loading soft drinks into a cold case. He nodded a greeting in my direction.

"Just looking for a cup of coffee," I said.

He jerked his thumb toward the area on my right.

"On the other side. Rebecca'll take care of you."

The room was L-shaped, the other section a lunch counter with a pass-through to the kitchen area. I stopped, studying the place. It looked as if it were left over from another era. Get rid of a few modern claptrap touches, and it could be a movie set—easy enough to imagine Henry Fonda here, doing a scene for *The Grapes of Wrath*.

The lunch counter was short, with a half-dozen stools. Opposite was a collection of mismatched chairs surrounding two battered tables. I pushed aside a pile of newspapers and sat down. Just then I heard a sudden scurry of movement in the kitchen, and the sound of a door closing.

I sorted through the newspapers—*San Francisco Chronicle* sports section, comic pages, a partly done crossword puzzle. Then I found Friday's *Fairville Reporter* folded open to a headline on the front page: Mystery Mummy in Old House. There was a four-column picture of the Queen Anne with stuff from under the porch all over the yard, and a caption under the photo saying the police were still investigating. I settled down with the article.

The subhead said, "Identity of Infant, Cause of Death, May Never Be Known." That was probably the gist of it, all right. "The mummified body of an infant girl was discovered by a Damien Enterprises construction worker...." They didn't have it altogether right. No matter—just as well, in fact. I was grateful not to see my name attached to the story. "An autopsy is to be performed, according to Solano County Coroner Alvin Gibson. All queries were referred by Fairville Police to the Coroner's office, which declined to release further information, except that an inquest will be scheduled."

They hadn't said a word about the wire I'd seen around the baby's neck. Standard procedure, I supposed—an advantage to be used when and if they ever turned up anybody to question.

The story mentioned a spokesperson for Damien Enterprises, who "declined specific comment, saying only that the discovery was made by a subcontractor." Well, that was right. "Construction of Victorian Villa will not be delayed. The project, scheduled for completion by the end of this year, will include..." It went on and on about plans for the Victorian Villa condo project. Typical small-town journalism: a crime story turned into publicity for a major advertiser.

"You get your coffee, lady?" The guy with the mustache was peering around the corner.

"No, I didn't," I said. "Your waitress must have stepped out for a few minutes."

Scowling, he walked over and looked into the empty kitchen. "Damn!" He headed for a spattered glass server that held a few inches of foul-looking stuff. "You take cream in your coffee?"

"That's all right," I said quickly. "I'll just wait until she comes back."

He hesitated by a stack of coffee mugs.

"Glad to pour it for you," he said, at the same time peering out the back door. "If she don't come back pretty quick..." He turned to me. "Say, you're looking at that story in the *Reporter*." He brightened considerably. "You know, that old house is right up the road from here."

"That so?" I said.

"Yeah.... There was a heck of a commotion up there."

"I guess there must have been," I said, trying to seem impressed.

He warmed up to the topic. "I had people coming in all that day and the next, asking what was going on up there. And you can see the place from here, from the kitchen. Christ! That dead baby under the porch all these years—spooky. Not that stuff like that bothers *me*."

"Of course not," I said quickly.

"It spooked Rebecca. You know, she's kinda funny about that old house."

"No kidding. Say, what do you know about that place?"

"Hell if I know much. I'm new here—just bought this business the first of July. It was real run-down, that other guy didn't know what you got to do to keep the customers happy. I been trying to upgrade ever since. Like right away I got in the ready-made sandwiches over on the grocery side. You know, the Seven-Elevens have 'em."

I nodded in agreement, as if that was the wisest improvement he could have made.

"Hey, you know what?" he said eagerly. "Rebecca could tell you about that house, she lived up there once."

"She did?" That was a surprise.

"Yeah, sure." He looked pleased at having some kind of link to an important event. "She sorta came with this place, Rebecca did." He glanced at the empty kitchen and his voice took on a confidential tone. "I *know* she knew something before they found that baby. She'd been asking the construction guys questions about what they're gonna do with the old house. And she said she had to take that afternoon off—before the baby was found.''

"You really think she knew something?''

"Hey.... What'd I tell you? She's been working here all this time, hasn't she?''

He sat down beside me with the air of a man about to reveal something significant. "I tell you, I know stuff. Couldn't tell the cops, though. Nothing you could put your finger on.''

"What do you know?'' I asked.

"I know a lot,'' he said, oozing self-importance. "That Rebecca's one nutty woman, I tell you.'' He tapped a finger to his forehead. "You know what I mean—not playing with a full deck. As far as I'm concerned, she needs a keeper. Used to live with her mother, she told me. But her mother's dead now, and she's started seeing some damn psychic, says he told her to watch over the house. A bunch of nonsense about she was going to learn something she's been waiting a long time to find out.''

By now I was certain Rebecca had been spying on me. Maybe she was the woman in the Karmann Ghia.

"I dunno what it is with her,'' the man with the handlebar mustache went on, "but I made up my mind yesterday to get me another waitress." He looked carefully around the restaurant. "I don't wanna say anything bad about Rebecca...." He looked around again, then leaned over and spoke in a whisper. "Between you and me, I think that might have been her baby."

He straightened, looking at me as if to see what I thought of his insider knowledge. "You think about it," he added. "Those were a bunch of hippies living up there."

He paused again. I nodded encouragement.

"Hippies." He leaned forward again. "Who knows what they used to do? Goings-on up there, you know what I mean, with drugs and all. If that baby wasn't Rebecca's,"—he looked over to check the empty kitchen one more time—"she knows who the mother is."

"You really think so?"

"Plain as the nose on your face."

He sat back with a satisfied expression.

"I didn't tell the cops, though. Let them do their homework about who lived there and whatever the hell went on." He shook his head. "Anyhow, there's nothing to tell, nothing you could put your finger on. I got my own problems. What if people start saying I got a nutty waitress here? Bad for business."

"I suppose so."

"She's got weird ideas, I tell you, with what that psychic con artist told her."

"You think she thought she was supposed to watch for...um...the person who found the baby?"

He shrugged. "Who knows? She's crazy. Like I told you, that woman's not playing with a full deck."

He got up and looked out the kitchen door.

"Say, I don't know what kind of bug bit Rebecca this time—she's sure as hell done a disappearing act. I'll get your coffee."

"I'm running out of time. Thanks anyway, for the chance to read your paper."

I climbed back into my truck, and then, on impulse, decided to circle through the cafe parking lot to turn around. At the back of the lot I noticed a carport, with an old-fashioned trumpet vine in full bloom growing over it. The blossoms were orange, just like the ones that used to cover my grandmother's back fence.

Inside the carport was the pumpkin-colored Karmann Ghia.

I stopped and jumped out of the truck to investigate. The car's engine abruptly started. The

Karmann Ghia backed out of the carport and, tires squealing, turned and sped out of the lot. Behind the wheel was the mousey-looking woman. Rebecca.

EIGHT

THE KARMANN GHIA spewed dust and gravel on its way out of the parking lot. Rebecca accelerated recklessly, fishtailing up the road toward the hills, and I followed, my own tires screeching.

This was insane. If we played this nonsense according to script, we'd be up in those hills and careening around corners as if we were acting out some kind of adolescent fantasy. What were we supposed to do, try to force each other off the road? I didn't want to play snuggle-fender games, which in this case would include taking the chance of plunging into one of those steep foothill canyons.

I was gaining a little on her. Up ahead was still a bit of straightaway. There was a big oak tree coming up on the left, and on the right a long clumpy row of what looked like poison oak bushes. There seemed to be room for what I had in mind. I was coming up fast on the Karmann Ghia and starting to move up beside it. I planned to pull alongside.

Rebecca hit the brakes hard and took a quick right turn, leaving me to shoot on past, braking for all I was worth, and heading into the first uphill curve.

It served me right, I suppose.

I had my hands full negotiating a series of curves as the road hairpinned up the steep ascent. There was no room on the shoulder to attempt a turnaround. I was almost to the top ridge before I found some extra space at an elbow in the road. I turned around and took it easy coming back down. No sense in speeding now. She'd had ample time to make good her escape.

I rounded the last curve and surveyed the straightaway ahead. Just this side of the poison oak bushes was the narrow side road onto which Rebecca had turned. A smart trick, but smart only in the short term. The man at the cafe knew what he was talking about when he said she wasn't playing with a full deck. She'd accomplished nothing, unless she planned to run away altogether. I knew where she worked and who she was. Well, I knew her first name was Rebecca.

I WENT BACK to have a talk with the cafe owner. He gave me a sharp look as I came in and perched on one of the stools at the counter. He said nothing—just settled in to looking at me, blank-faced.

Deliberately so, I thought. I waited to see what he'd say. It was a standoff at first, but he finally broke the silence.

"You some kind of bill collector?"

"No."

"No kidding."

His tone was flat, disbelieving. He said nothing more. I decided to wait again.

"Where did you two go?" he said at last.

"I was trying to catch up to her, but she took a fast right by that oak tree."

"Yeah."

He turned back to working in the kitchen. I watched as he loaded hamburger patties out of the freezer. Maybe he was feeling uncomfortable about all the talking about Rebecca he'd done before.

"Guess I gotta get the stuff ready myself," he said after a long while. "Sundays are slow, but we get some regulars for the dinner trade."

Maybe he was starting to loosen up a little, I thought. Then he gave me another of those sharp looks.

"You sure you're not a bill collector?"

"No way. It was a big surprise to me, when she took off like that."

"It was, huh."

He studied me, cold-eyed. I gave it one more try.

"You said her name's Rebecca. What's her last name?"

His expression had hardened—a flat, angry look. I thought he wasn't going to answer me.

"Higgins," he said finally. "Rebecca Higgins."

He turned his back then and put on a show of paying attention to his work. He hadn't wanted to tell me her name. He resented me for getting it out of him, and probably for coming around in the first place—as if I'd twisted his arm to make him say all those things about Rebecca.

There was nothing more to be gained here. I headed over to the new Damien Enterprises shopping center.

BELLE HAD DUBBED the place Palladium. Everything was white and blue, the theme classic Grecian. It had been followed relentlessly. A double row of olive trees flanked the entrance; inside, the place was loaded with columns, bas-relief murals, and statues on pedestals. Interior storefronts—all looking like the Parthenon—lined a spacious walkway with a faux stone floor. More olive trees, planted in urns, led to a huge central courtyard. Here was the reflecting pond Frannie had carried on about. A pièce de résistance for sure, with water lilies in bloom floating about, its surface mirroring the ceiling high above on which blue sky and fluffy clouds had been painted.

Belle must have shelled out a parcel of money for this. Just like a developer, I thought. Tear out the real landscape and then spend a bundle imitating nature, just to bring in people to spend more money.

Handsome waiters in tuxedos and caterers' maids in little black ruffled dresses scuttled around, serving wine and hors d'oeuvres from silver trays. I walked through the crowd of glitzy people who were busy seeing and being seen. Before long I'd spotted Belle, decked out in a dress of silver lamé and big chunks of what looked like real lapis lazuli. Frannie was with Belle's group— Whitaker, too, beaming a smile that was turned up to full wattage.

I felt kind of proud, watching Frannie. She had on a new outfit, salmon and white, a Filipina-style dress with a long skirt and wide elbow-length sleeves puffed at the shoulder. She looked terrific—every bit as terrific as *La Belle Damien*.

Signor Gigolo Whitaker was something else in sharply creased, pale gray slacks, a double-breasted dark blazer with wide lapels and brass buttons—and, for God's sake, a paisley ascot. I watched him for a while. He seemed never to stop smiling, even when it looked as if there was nothing in particular to smile about.

Then I noticed a man who didn't seem to be part of the socialite group around Belle. He'd shown up at her side and she'd given him her attention immediately. They pulled back from the others. I don't know what gave me a certain feeling about the guy. He was maybe forty, wearing a dark suit and tie, with nothing special about his looks. I thought he might be a security type, but he didn't look like a private policeman in civilian clothes— he had more the aura of one of those Secret Service men who guard big-time politicians. His conversation with Belle was brief, after which he melted back into the crowd.

Now what was that all about?

Frannie spotted me. She waved, signalling me to come over and join her. I waved back, but indicated I was going in the other direction. By this time I'd caught sight of a side courtyard, and Clara's watercolors.

The display—Clara's stuff and the Indian baskets—was impressive. The effect was heightened by the vista beyond. A row of big glass doors led out to a patio and a terrific view of the nearby hillsides, an unspoiled panorama of golden grass and dark green oak.

Clara's watercolors were surprisingly large. Mounted on free-standing clear plastic panels, they were arranged in a row leading toward the glass doors—a group of landscapes of the local scenery, showing the area as it must have looked before the white folks got here. There were marshlands with great swarms of ducks and geese flying overhead, Indian villages along willow-lined creeks, a herd of tule elk, a ceremony with Indian dancers in feather capes and deerskins. The series of scenes ended with a huge landscape—apparently created just for this show—picturing a hillside that exactly matched the view outside. Good art, I thought—and great showmanship.

Clara spotted me right away and came over. I told her I thought her stuff was terrific. She looked terrific, too. She'd let her dusky blonde hair grow long and straight. She wore no makeup. She didn't need it, with her creamy skin and those thick, dark lashes setting off her clear brown eyes. When I mentioned how good she looked, she almost blushed. What a switch! The high-school-days' Clara with the punk getup would have been so *cool* she wouldn't have admitted to any emo-

tion, but the new Clara was unabashedly enthusiastic.

"I got a grant from the country arts commission to render the area as it once looked. But this
was something I wanted to do anyway, you know,
sort of raise people's consciousness about the environment."

"It's terrific," I said. "The way this countryside is getting torn up nowaday..."

Clara interrupted me.

"I want you to meet someone."

A dusky-skinned young woman with jet black
hair had approached. She obviously belonged with
the collection of Indian baskets, which were dis-
played on long tables arranged on each side of
Clara's pictures.

"This is Judy Moore," Clara told me.

Judy shook my hand. She was good-looking,
with broad cheekbones and a round face, and the
squarish, short-waisted build so typical of local
tribes—but slender. She seemed shy at first, and
then seemed to make a deliberate effort to switch
to a different persona. She turned on a nervous
eagerness, explaining the finer points of each basket.

A sales pitch. She didn't have to do that—not
with me—and she must have known it. Why the

hard-sell number? There was some kind of crusade—they were, after all, selling baskets to raise money. I studied the baskets, only half-listening to Judy's pitch. Some were antique, but there were new ones, too. I'd always thought that the people who had the skill to make really fine baskets had died out.

"My aunt makes them," Judy said, as if reading my mind.

Judy's aunt must be one hell of a basket maker, I thought. Baskets like this—fine strands woven so tight they'd hold water—take a chunk of time to make. They're a big item with collectors, and I realized there was a lot of money in Indian baskets sitting around here.

"These older baskets have never been on the market before," Judy volunteered. "But now..." She glanced over her shoulder, still nervous. "We're using them to raise money. We..."

She and Clara exchanged glances.

"I wish my husband Charlie could have been here today," Judy said suddenly. "You might..." There was another quick glance toward Clara. "Well.... I wanted you to meet Charlie."

"I was going to tell her anyway," Clara said to Judy. "Oh, hello, Aunt Frannie."

Frannie was standing beside me.

"Aren't these baskets beautiful?" Clara said right away. "Judy's aunt makes them."

Frannie dutifully complimented Judy on the baskets, and then made her usual kind of small talk—but not for long.

"Emma," she said, "we're all waiting for you. Everybody wants you to come over. You know.... About what you found."

How had that come out? Now I'd have to let her drag me back to chitchat with Lord-knows-who, about something I didn't think belonged in the chitchat category.

I told Clara again how much I liked her watercolors and then—still keeping Frannie waiting— told Judy I hoped I'd have a chance to learn more about the baskets.

"Tell you what," I said to Clara as Frannie took me in tow, "I'll give you a call."

"Clara's artwork is beautiful," I said as Frannie headed us back to Belle Damien's circle. "I'm looking forward to learning more about what she's doing—her artwork, I mean."

We rejoined Belle's group. It soon became apparent that Frannie hadn't been able to resist the temptation to tell people it was her friend who had found the baby. I had become, in some weird way, a celebrity. Belle and I were introduced. She had obviously made the connection between *Frannie Edmundson's friend* and *the woman from A-1 Salvage*.

I made awkward conversation, at the same time mulling over the all-too-pat connections to the dead baby: the initials on the cradle and the Damien pickup at the old Queen Anne.

NINE

As I WAS TRYING to disengage myself from the conversation with Belle, I noticed startled looks and sudden silences travel away from me in ever-expanding circles. Word was spreading that I was the one who had found the dead baby.

I watched as the information reached Whitaker. He'd apparently found someone else to practice his smile on as soon as Frannie had left him to fetch me—a little dried-up-looking woman with gobs of makeup and bright auburn hair. He turned slowly and stared at me, with a look that reminded me of nothing so much as the way a snake fixes its eyes on a mouse it's about to have for supper. He soon hustled over.

"You lovely ladies never cease to amaze me," he said to me, affecting a tone halfway between funeral director and quiz show emcee. "I had no idea you were in the salvage business."

I did my best not to show my distaste for the man, or for that smile, which he'd quickly brought up to full wattage again. I knew that behind that pasted-on charm was the realization that I wasn't just another foolish old woman. If he wanted to get at Frannie's money, he was going to have to get past me to do it.

Fine, I thought. It might give me some satisfaction to watch him try.

I made my escape soon afterward, eager to be home and have some time to myself to mull over the day's events.

SOURPUSS WAS WAITING for me at the top of the steps and followed me inside. He rubbed back and forth at my ankles, meowing continuously. I fished a plate of leftover roast chicken out of the refrigerator.

"Come on," I said. "You and I are going to have some dead bird." I pulled off a wing for him. "You have no idea of the day I've had. I was out playing spy-novel games—flunked my first big chase scene, too."

After I'd gotten out of my fancy clothes, I loaded some chicken on a plate for myself, got out a piece of bread and an apple to go with it, and took my dinner out on the porch. I ate standing up, leaning on the railing to enjoy the first of the evening breezes and turning my thoughts to Rebecca.

She'd been seeing a psychic, and apparently believed some crazy prediction. I wondered if she'd

known the baby was under the verandah at the old
Queen Anne. Maybe she hoped it would be discovered, and the police would go after whoever
did it. No, that didn't add up. She could have gone
to the police long ago. She'd followed me the day
I found the baby, then run away. Today she'd run
away again. There was no explanation, except *not
playing with a full deck*. Or *inexplicable*.

I decided to forget the whole thing and go for a
walk.

It was twilight as I set out, eager for a stretch of
the legs, and for a look at what was in bloom here
and there in our neighborhood. I didn't expect to
find much. A few days of that north wind can de-
stroy more flowers than a spring hailstorm. I
headed for one of my favorite spots, a big house
with blue Lilies of the Nile bordering the drive.
They'd withstood the heat pretty well. Farther on,
in a neighborhood park, was a splendid display of
dwarf dahlia.

The dahlia's purples and oranges and yellows
were fading with the last of the daylight. It was
time to start home. I'd just turned the corner onto
our street when I spotted a cat I'd never seen in the
neighborhood before—a sleek black shorthair,
hardly more than a kitten. She was sitting next to

a hydrangea bush that filled the space under a bay window, not keeping to the shadows the way cats usually do, but perched primly in the light from a street lamp. I settled myself on a low cement balustrade by the sidewalk and started my usual sweet-talking routine, in hopes of getting a chance to pet her. The little cat, eyes intent on me, moved her ears and tilted her head—and stayed right where she was.

I picked up a twig and scratched it lightly on the cement. She made a little start in my direction. I scratched again, and she trotted right over. The distraction had worked; she forgot all about caution and let me scoop her up and cuddle her in my lap as if we were old friends.

Maybe Rebecca didn't have much more sense than this cat. Maybe it made no sense to look for logic in what she did; perhaps she really wanted to talk to me, but was plain scared. Maybe I could just find a way to scoop her up, so to speak, and gain her confidence.

It was a long shot, to be sure, and I'd have to have a go at it pretty quick. The new detective—Holmes—would probably want everyone in the neighborhood of the old house questioned. If Rebecca was afraid of *me*, a police interview would probably give her a real scare. All of this, of course, was assuming she'd report back to work at the cafe.

I'd make it my business to find out tomorrow.

TEN

THE NEXT DAY, before I headed for Fairville, I took time out to call Clara to find out what was going on with her and Judy Moore. I got right to the point and asked why Judy had been so nervous and mysterious.

"It's just that she was uptight," Clara said. "For her, being in Belle Damien's shopping center was like being in the enemy camp."

"The Palladium was a bit much, wasn't it? But it seemed to me Belle had gone out of her way to help you two."

"Yes, but Judy doesn't like developers—doesn't trust them."

Amen, I thought.

"You know, up at the Madrone *rancheria*, she and Charlie have started a project. They want to make things better for the tribe—keep out big real estate developers, create jobs that will do some good for people. Not just go-nowhere jobs, like working at that bingo place. Things have been pretty bad up there. You know what most of the *rancherias* are like.... People giving up hope, living on welfare.''

"Selling baskets is going to fix all this?''

"It's a start, one way to raise money. You see, Charlie's got a plan. Raising capital with the baskets is just the first part of it.''

She went on, talking a mile a minute. They'd start businesses, give jobs to people at the *rancheria*, preserve the environment.

"We can make it work, I know we can. Judy's so proud of Charlie. She'd given up on her heritage, you know, left the *rancheria*. She was living in Seattle when she met Charlie. If he hadn't decided to look around for a new place to start a river raft business, she would never have—''

"Whoa!'' I said. "Slow down. Give it to me from the place that starts, 'Meanwhile, back at the *rancheria*.'''

I found out that Judy and her husband had started a corporation, Ventures Unlimited. They had several endeavors going—a basketmaking cooperative, a wild rice harvesting enterprise, raft trips on Trapper Creek—but the idea went beyond jobs and economic independence. Judy and Charlie were fearful of development on or near Indian land, especially since outsiders had come in and set up the high-stakes bingo operation.

"Charlie says that not only do we have to create our own companies," Clara told me, "we have to raise capital to buy land. Outsiders are only interested in exploitation. They'll exploit the tribe and the land."

Now she was giving me a sales pitch, the same way Judy had, with words no doubt borrowed from Charlie. I wondered if Belle's future plans might include some development around the *rancheria*.

"I haven't got time to explain it all now," Clara said suddenly. "Emma, I want to ask a favor."

"What would that be?"

"Oh, I think you'll like it," Clara said. "If you can spare a day, would you like to come along on a river trip?"

"When?"

"Wednesday. I thought of you right away when Charlie said he needed a volunteer crew. This will be a demonstration run for some official from B.I.A., and he thinks he's got a reporter from the *New York Times* interested, too."

Charlie was one smart cookie. Start with the Bureau of Indian Affairs, and add a little free publicity in a major national newspaper.

"Sure, I'll go, but don't some of the men from the tribe want to...."

"Not really," Clara said with exasperation. "It's because of the bingo operation. It's so... debilitating. Every family gets a monthly dole from them. Now the men just drink beer and ride around in their trucks, and the kids think it's bigtime to work for minimum wage in the bingo parlor. You see what we're up against?"

"I get the drift. You said Charlie needed a volunteer crew?"

"Two people. Do you know someone else who might come?"

"Sure."

Joe would say yes, I was certain.

Clara said she'd call the next day when she knew the details.

As soon as our conversation was finished, I started to call Joe, but hung up when I heard a knock on my door, and peeked out my kitchen window to see who it was.

Vince.

I had little choice but to open the door and invite him in. He stepped inside, blushing and stammering, apparently embarrassed at being in my apartment without a chaperone.

"You're sure I'm not—I don't want to interrupt you or anything."

"No problem, Vince. I have to go somewhere pretty quick, but I've got a few minutes."

I cleared the morning newspaper off my little kitchen table and invited him to sit down.

"Emma, you remember I said I knew Clem Miller?"

"Sure. The rental agent."

"He told me who lived in the place."

Vince fished in his shirt pocket and brought out a notebook. He thumbed through the pages.

"I got it all down here somewhere."

Vince put the open notebook down on the table and tapped it with a stubby finger.

"Bill Smith."

"What else?"

"Just the name, no other ID."

Great, I thought. The guy might just as well have signed as John Doe.

"Lease signed by Bill Smith, the rent paid in cash. No problems in collecting rent."

"But the Damiens had the tenants evicted."

"Yeah. It was a bunch of hippies living there."

He'd come all the way to Sacramento just to tell me this?

"We checked out the rest of that house."

"Oh?"

"Whoever it was, they only got into one bedroom upstairs. Not much there. We found some old phonograph records, a plastic Christmas tree, a bathing suit—"

"A man's or a woman's?"

"Woman's."

Had this been Rebecca's room?

"There were old magazines, too, and a shoebox full of snapshots. Those were scattered all over."

"I wonder what they were looking for—maybe evidence that would link that person to whoever lived in the room."

"Yeah."

Vince chortled.

"What's so funny?"

"That smarty-pants Holmes. He's running around in circles about the photographs, trying to put together some theory about what kind of person they belonged to. And that's *after* someone came and took all the ones that might show anything.

"No harm," I said. "Sounds like he's really digging into this."

"Yeah." Vince was fishing around in his shirt pocket again. "I brought you something else."

"What's that?"

"There was an old copy of the *Fairville Reporter* up there in the hallway. Part of the front page was torn off. This morning Holmes sent me over to the newspaper office to get the rest of the page." He grinned with eager pride. "I brought you a copy. And you know what? It was tore off on purpose." It took him a while to spread out the tightly folded copy of the newspaper page and carefully smooth out the creases.

"See? Down here."

He'd circled an item on the bottom of the page. Someone named Nancy Teagarden had been arrested for possession of marijuana and several pills. The address she'd given was the same as the Queen Anne.

"Not much," Vince said, "but I wanted to bring it to you first, before I reported back to Holmes."

The visit with me was Old Lonely's real objective, but I thanked him.

Maybe, I thought, Rebecca hadn't lived in the room. Maybe it had been Nancy Teagarden, whoever she was. I was disappointed. I wanted a nice, tidy package, evidence that Rebecca had lived at the Queen Anne.

"At least," I said, "Nancy Teagarden sounds more like someone's real name than Bill Smith."

"I was on the force when those hippies were up at that old house," Vince said. "We had a couple of drug complaints, but nothing you could hang your hat on, so far as this case is concerned. And Holmes—I know he's gonna make me dig out the old files, every one of them."

"Maybe you'll turn up something."

Vince squirmed and looked around the room, as though he were trying to think of something to say to prolong the visit.

"Nice place you got here." His gaze settled on my coffee pot. "Real nice place."

I stood up.

"Thanks for coming by, Vince. I've really got to be going now."

"Aw . . . Say, you on your way to work? Maybe I could help you out for a little while."

"Thanks for the offer, but—"

I felt sorry for Vince, but not so sorry that I wasn't trying to think of something to send him on his way.

"Vince, I have a favor to ask."

He brightened immediately.

"Sure. Anything."

I told him about the man I'd seen talking to Belle at the shopping center and asked him to see what he could find out. He was as pleased as a puppy dog to be doing something for me.

"I'll get on it right away. Soon's I find out anything, I'll come back and tell you first thing."

Now I'd done it, I realized, given him another excuse for a visit—but at least I'd managed to get him out of my hair for now.

As soon as Vince had left, I phoned Joe—who was delighted at the prospect of the raft trip on Trapper Creek—and then left for Fairville.

ELEVEN

By the time I'd gotten to Fairville it was 11:30, not a good time to try to have a talk with a waitress. I decided I might as well go on a little fishing expedition.

I drove to the Damien Enterprises' corporate lair—a multistoried building in a fancy new business park not far from Palladium. The building was art deco, rendered in concrete with pearl gray trim and a touch of crimson here and there. It loomed over the parking lot, since it was by far the tallest structure in the area. Ostentatious, by my lights, designed to impress the smithereens out of ordinary folk. I stood in the lobby, knowing I looked out of place in my khaki pants and work shirt, and scanned the directory. Belle's personal office suite occupied the entire third floor.

The elevator opened into a large room decked out with potted palms, aggressively modern, with just about everything except the palms done up in either pearl gray or crimson. A clone of the woman who'd met me at the old house sat at a desk shaded by the biggest palm in the room. She gave me a look of mild surprise.

"May I help you?"

"I'm Emma Chizzit. A-1 Salvage."

I could see that didn't ring any bells—and wasn't likely to open any doors.

"I found.... That is, last week I was the one working in that old house at Victorian Villa. I have a reason for wanting to contact the former tenants. I was wondering if you might be able to look up who lived there."

Belle had already told the police she knew nothing, but I thought there was no harm at having a go at it from a different direction. The clone began slowly shaking her head from side to side; maybe she'd been given orders to reveal nothing. I kept on, before she could say *no* out loud.

"Surely you could check for information about who lived there."

"I'm not authorized to release company records on any matter."

"Before all the excitement started, I found a small item of furniture under the porch. I'm interested in tracing the owner."

I was favored with a blank look.

"Maybe you can tell me when the house was purchased," I said, just to have something else to ask.

Another blank look.

"I know it was sold by the Jorgensen family to Damien Enterprises."

"I'm sorry, but..."

"Real estate transactions are a matter of public record. All I'm asking is that you save me the bother of looking it up."

I congratulated myself for thinking of this ploy, and was wondering what I could try next, when Belle herself saved me the trouble.

"Miss Pomeroy, it's all right. I'll be pleased to talk to Mrs. Chizzit."

She walked toward me, graciousness personified, her hand extended. Then she led the way to her inner sanctum, a large room filled with table-top models of various Damien developments. An oversize desk occupied a glass-walled alcove. Belle sat down, facing me across its wide expanse.

"What can I do for you?"

Belle sounded calm and poised, but she played nervously with one of her expensive desktop doo-dads. I sat up straighter and leaned forward, hoping to take advantage of being taller than Belle.

Maybe she thought I was trying to snoop at something on her desk. One hand made an almost imperceptible movement, as if to ward off my scrutiny, and then she had her psychological armor on again.

"As I told your assistant," I said, "I'd like to contact whoever lived in the house."

"The rental information has been turned over to the police." A tight little smile. "I'm sure they'll be checking into that."

"You've owed the house for a long time, and kept it boarded up after—" I caught myself. I'd almost let on what I'd learned from Vince. "Well, I just thought you might remember something about the tenants."

"I had no personal contact with the tenants. I'm sorry that Miss Pomeroy was a bit stuffy with you," she offered, changing the subject.

"It sounded to me as if your secretary was only doing her job. I know she's not supposed to give out information to just anybody. But I have a reason for wanting to know who lived there. I found something . . ."

"Yes. I heard."

There was an edge of eagerness in her voice. So that's what had brought her out to talk to me.

"I'm quite curious," Belle went on. "Do you mind telling me what you found?"

I felt like I was giving away the store. I should have been holding back and trying to get something out of her, but I'd run out of questions.

"I found a cradle, all dismantled and packed away. I put it in my truck when I first started working there."

Judging by her lack of reaction, if Belle *had* been worried that I'd found something in particular, this didn't seem to be it—but I wondered how she'd react when I told her about the initials.

"I forgot about the cradle at first, in all the excitement. I remembered it later and brought it in to the police."

Belle shifted slightly in her chair. Was she getting ready to end the interview?

"The cradle seemed sort of special to me," I said. "It's an antique, and I thought the original owner might really want it, what with the initials on it and all."

"What initials were on the cradle?"

"*A*," I said. "And *D*."

No response.

"I was wondering if that cradle might have belonged to someone in the Damien family."

"I'm well acquainted with the Damien family history. I can assure you, there is no family member with those initials."

"There isn't?"

She smiled, just a bit.

"There's no one with the initials *AD* in the Damien family. At least, no one . . . no one in the last three generations."

She was telling the truth. I'd bet on it.

"Scout's honor," she added, with a self-conscious smile.

"I guess I was just too wound up in this thing," I said. "I gave in to the temptation to play detective."

I felt better, going ahead and admitting it. There was no reason why I should play the game the way she did. Maybe that defensive exterior of hers had made me crawl into a shell of my own, when I didn't need to.

"I'm not surprised at your interest," Belle said. "Finding that baby's corpse—that's not something I'd want to encounter."

Her sympathy seemed genuine. For the first time I tried to picture her reaction when she'd heard the news. No one wants to discover they own a house with a dead baby in it, least of all someone like Belle who has to stand up to a lot of

public scrutiny—and doesn't want any negative
publicity to hinder sales.

"The news must have come as quite a shock to
you, too," I said.

She didn't answer.

"Well," I went on, "I guess I'll just have to
leave the detective business to the police."

"Indeed."

Her tone was decidedly cool. *La Belle Damien*
had retreated back into her corporate-image shell.

"With all the difficulties over this," she went
on, "I'm sure you'll be wanting some payment
right away for your work."

Belle must have signaled over some kind of in-
tercom. Her secretary appeared, notebook in
hand.

"Miss Pomeroy, see that Mrs. Chizzit receives
a check for half the contract amount before she
leaves today. And make certain she's paid immediately when she presents a bill for the completed
work."

"Certainly, Mrs. Damien." The secretary
paused, then made a gesture with the notebook.
"You have an urgent call, from . . ."

She stopped to glance at the notebook. Belle's
attention was distracted. I edged forward, trying
for a quick look at her desk top.

"The call's from Mr. Dimitri, of Bell, Hodges, and Dopkins."

"I'll talk to Mr. Dimitri in just a moment."

I'd caught sight of Belle's appointment calendar, with several typed items on the page that I couldn't read. I did see something very curious though. Scrawled in bold red handwriting was a single word: Oracle.

TWELVE

I DROVE ON OVER to the cafe as soon as I'd left Belle's office, anxious to discover whether Rebecca was there.

I was convinced Belle had been telling the truth when she said no one in the Damien family had the initials *AD*, but I was equally convinced that she was trying to hide *something*.

The word Oracle hadn't indicated a routine appointment scheduled by Belle's assistant, but had been hastily scrawled, probably by Belle. It struck me that a psychic might set up in business under that name, but that was nonsense. My imagination was working overtime, ready to jump at any straw to connect Belle and Rebecca and the baby.

I again parked down the street from the cafe. As I strolled slowly toward it, I noticed a Damien pickup parked up the street. No need to get spooked about that. I had to keep the old imagination in rein. This was the nearest place for Victorian Villa workers to come for lunch.

I checked the cafe parking lot. It was nearly empty, just the last few cars for the lunch trade. As

I got closer, I took a look in the carport. The Karmann Ghia was there. If Rebecca was really trying to hide from me, it was illogical that she'd come back, but no surprise. Not playing with a full deck was what the man had said.

I entered the cafe quietly, taking care not to let the screen door bang. The confidence I'd had last night, when I'd connected Rebecca's behavior to the little black kitty's, was beginning to evaporate. Just take hold of her by the shoulders, I'd told myself, settle her down, and convince her she needn't be afraid of me. Now the idea seemed downright dumb.

The owner was busy ringing up cold drinks and prepackaged sandwiches for some men in coveralls. He didn't even glance up. I sidled over to the bend of the L-shaped room and ventured a look. Four construction workers had apparently just come in and were settling themselves at one of the battered tables. They were the only restaurant customers, except for another worker on one of the counter stools.

Rebecca was there, her back to me. She was down at the far end of the counter, filling water glasses.

"Hey, 'Becca," one of the men at the table hollered. "Bring a menu this time." He winked at the others. "I wanna see what you got."

The men guffawed.

"Just hold your horses, Lester."

I moved silently, intending to be in a position to head Rebecca off if she started for the kitchen. Still unaware that I was there, she loaded three water glasses into her left hand, then picked up a fourth with her right.

"Rebecca," I said.

She turned toward me, a smile on her face.

The smile froze, the water glasses crashed to the floor. She lit out, pushing right past me.

"Wait!" I yelped. I tried to get to her before she escaped through the kitchen, but the floor was slippery with ice and water. "Wait!"

She flew out the kitchen door, with me right after her. I ignored the commotion in the restaurant behind us, concentrating on catching up to Rebecca. I was close enough that she wasn't going to make it to her car—or, at worst, I'd catch up to her while she was still getting into it.

I wasn't aware what the loud, sharp sound was, just that Rebecca had stumbled and fallen.

We were both on the ground then, Rebecca under me, screaming, clutching at her middle. I was so close behind that I'd fallen practically on top of her.

It's a miracle I wasn't hit when the second shot came.

I looked up and saw a man crouching by the carport, holding a revolver with both hands, just like in the movies. He was dressed in construction worker clothes, blue jeans and a hooded sweatshirt, but the clothes were new and clean, and the drawstring on the hood was pulled tight so that it was up over his chin and down almost to his eyebrows. He wore a pair of aviator-style dark glasses, too. Almost nothing was visible of his face.

An instant later, he had fled. Men from the restaurant were behind me, yelling.

I scrambled to my hands and knees beside Rebecca. She was whimpering and squirming, bent over almost double. On the dusty gravel of the parking lot, a puddle of blood grew beside her. She was badly injured—my God!—maybe dying.

"Get an ambulance!"

I didn't turn around to see if anyone went running for the phone. I was too busy trying to remember what I'd learned about first aid. Blood was coming from her stomach, flowing over her hands and spreading slowly over the gravel. There was nothing I could do to stop that kind of bleeding.

"Get an ambulance," I screamed again.

All I could do for Rebecca was offer comfort. I reached out to her, touched her forehead, tried to smooth back her hair. Her face was rigid with pain, her eyes tightly shut.

"Rebecca . . ."

She opened her eyes and brought one blood-smeared hand away from her middle to stare at it.

"I'm so sorry, Rebecca." It was my fault. If I hadn't come into the cafe, if she hadn't run out here, she'd still be back there exchanging banter with the construction workers. "I didn't mean . . ."

She looked at me, then back at her hand, then at me again. I tried to keep my eyes on hers, not look at the blood.

She was trying to say something. I leaned forward.

"What?"

"You . . . took . . ."

Her voice trailed off.

I looked around, frantic. One of the men was in the phone booth, gesturing wildly. I bent to her again.

"You . . . took . . . grandmother's . . ."

Blood was smeared all over, seeping through her waitress uniform.

I wrenched my eyes away from the spreading stain and leaned closer. Her eyes were rolled away from me now, and she squirmed feebly, but the tension was going out of her face. It was turning pasty white, relaxed, and soft.

She looked straight at me, seeming to be making an effort to hold on to consciousness.

"Do you know who did this to you, Rebecca?"

Her eyeballs swivelled toward where the man had stood, and her lips moved in an effort to speak, then she started to gasp—shallow, shuddering breaths. Her mouth opened, closed, opened again. There was a slight change of expression in her eyes, a miniscule movement, as if she were trying to look right into my mind, a last effort to convey something.

Her eyes lost focus and slowly went vacant.

THIRTEEN

SOMEBODY CAME UP behind me and took me by the shoulders.

"Lady..."

He urged me backwards.

"Don't look, lady."

Her eyes were blank, open, and staring.

"Somebody cover her up. Please, somebody cover her up."

"Come *on* lady."

He pulled me back farther, turned me away from Rebecca, and put his arm around my shoulders.

"Oh God! Cover her up!"

He turned my face toward his chest. I didn't want to see. They were all looking, staring at me, staring at Rebecca. As he moved me away, he kept asking if I was all right. Then I was left to myself, to stand numbly in front of the wash basin in the cafe's grubby little rest room. I don't know how long I stood there before I finally began to get myself under control.

I heard sirens. Police, maybe an ambulance—I knew it didn't make any difference. The only illumination in the dim room filtered through the scummy glass of one high window; I didn't want to turn on the light. I ran my hands through my hair, then peered in the mirror. The backing on it had started to come away in spots. In my reflected image there was no difference between the spots in the mirror and the smears and spatters of blood on me. I shut my eyes and saw again Rebecca's blood, the way it had spread on her uniform.

My fault. I'd chased her out into that parking lot.

I ran water, splashed some on my face, combed my hair with my hands again. I've always liked to think I'm one tough old cookie, pretty much able to take an emotional jolt. I guess I'm not. I knew I was slow coming around, not doing well at getting myself together. It had all happened so fast.

Someone knocked at the door.

"Lady . . . you okay?"

You okay? I kept hearing those words. *You okay?*

I'd have to leave the rest room, but I wouldn't look up at those curious bystanders. I kept my eyes glued to the ground and allowed myself to be loaded into a police car, then unloaded again and ushered down a hallway.

You okay?

I KNEW PEOPLE meant well. I had to respond ... look up and notice where I was, collect myself once and for all. By now I was sitting in a small room, somebody's office, waiting to give my statement. I stood up and went over to look out the window.

This was a heck of a way, I thought, to meet Emerson Holmes for the first time.

He came striding into the room, carrying an expensive briefcase. Holmes was polished, very polished, a lean and rather sharp-looking young man, with pale olive skin and brown, slicked-back hair. He wore a dark summer suit, white shirt, and shiny dark tie.

He didn't ask if I was okay—just set down the briefcase and stuck out his hand.

"Emerson Holmes."

We shook hands, and then he opened the briefcase and took out a notepad. His brisk voice and smooth manner seemed to be announcing that our session would be all business. Formal. No untidy emotions.

Maybe he thought that was the best way to do things. His first day on the job he wouldn't want to cope with an old woman who'd weep all over him. I could understand that, but his imperious style got my goat.

"I realize this is not your first contact with our department, Mrs. Chizzit, but let's begin at the beginning, shall we?"

He started at the top of the page. Date. My name and address. Maybe this was what they had taught him when he was getting that fancy degree Vince had mentioned. Ask the witness routine questions first, no matter what.

A woman's just been killed, mister.

More questions.

"You have all that stuff," I said. "From the day I found the baby."

He stopped writing and glanced up at me. I'd sounded more hard-boiled than I'd meant to.

"We could start with what happened this afternoon," I said, more in my normal tone of voice. "And then I'll tell you why I called earlier and scheduled an appointment with you."

It went a little better after that. He was a little sticky about why I hadn't said right away about being followed by Rebecca, or about the stunt she'd pulled, running away and giving me the slip. I was going to report the incident, I said. How was I to know what would happen today? Up until now, there'd been only a long-ago unsolved murder and a skittish waitress. All I'd been going on was a hunch that Rebecca was linked to the baby. I'd had no idea someone would shoot her.

He kept on taking notes about everything I said.

I hemmed and hawed about how I hadn't wanted to mention this to Vince, but was waiting for *him* to take over the case. He turned stiffer than ever, but at least he didn't put this down in his notes.

When we were all through, he wouldn't offer any opinion about the initials on the cradle—or about anything, as far as that went. I understood the game plan. I was supposed to tell him everything; he would tell me nothing.

Debbie interrupted us. Several news reporters were waiting to talk to Holmes. He looked annoyed—or was it apprehensive?

"Mrs. Hughes," Holmes said, "tell the reporters I'll be with them momentarily. I want to have a few more words with—" He looked at me. "No, wait. I'll go out there now and finish talking with Mrs. Chizzit later. Maybe you should take her, and ... um ..." he waved an arm rather helplessly at me, "give her some assistance."

I still looked a mess, I realized.

Debbie took me down the hall to a rest room. We used cold water and paper towels to try to get the bloodstains out of my clothes.

"Are you all right?" Debbie asked when we'd finished.

I managed a grin.

"You're about the ten-thousandth person to ask."

I checked myself in the mirror. My shirt was water-splotched, but otherwise I looked pretty much my usual self.

"I guess I'm okay. I'm just used-up—ready to go home."

"Holmes still wants to talk to you. I guess it would be okay if you waited in the employee lounge."

She peeked into the hallway. I caught a glimpse of a television newsman with a camera hurrying by.

"Golly," she said.

News vultures. Debbie was still peeking out the door.

"Now!"

She hurried me down the hallway and through a doorway marked Employees Only.

The first thing I saw was Vince, sitting on a small couch and looking miserable. When he saw me, he leaped to his feet.

"Emma," he shouted. "Are you all right?"

Vince, obviously upset, was all over me with questions, at the same time bawling me out for keeping things from him, for not letting him help. I could have been killed, he kept saying.

He was right. Until now I hadn't thought about that.

"For Pete's sake, Emma, even a lady like you needs someone to protect her. You shouldn't have gone over there by yourself. You got *me*—why didn't you *tell* me?"

He had been pacing up and down. Now he stopped and stood facing me.

"You can't keep on doing stuff like this, not all by yourself." He put two heavy hands on my shoulders. "You got to let me drive you home."

Lord! The last thing I wanted!

"Vince," Debbie said quickly, "Emma can't leave just yet."

He looked crestfallen.

"But her truck is still over at the cafe." She turned to me. "Or at least, I suppose it is."

"It's still there," I said, "as far as I know."

"Vince, maybe you could take someone with you and go over to pick it up."

I handed my keys over to him, and in a minute he'd gone. I sank onto the little sofa.

"Thanks, Debbie," I said. "You're a peach."

She flashed me a wry grin.

"Well, Vince is . . ."

"Yeah." I shook my head. "He's really a nice man, but . . ."

She nodded. "Nicest guy in the world. He drives us all crazy."

Holmes came in.

"Mrs. Hughes," he said to Debbie, "people from the news media are still arriving. I've sent them all out front to wait. I want you to stay at the desk. Don't give out any information, just say I'll have a prepared statement shortly."

He looked unhappy. Some baptism by fire, I thought, for his first day on the job.

"Should have done that in the first place," he muttered.

"Baptism by fire," I said.

"What?"

"Never mind."

He looked considerably less cool and contained than when I first saw him.

"Do you need anything else from me? I'd like to go home."

"I've got to prepare a statement," he said, still talking as much to himself as to me.

I told him Vince was picking up my truck, and that I'd like to leave as soon as he'd brought it back. He cautioned me to remain available; he'd have further questions to ask me later.

"I'm not giving out your name. If any of those reporters track you down, I strongly advise you not to talk to them. As a matter of fact, I'd rather you didn't discuss this with anyone."

With that, he left. Vince arrived, my truck keys in hand, eager to take me home. I wouldn't let him, though it took a lot of talking. I prevailed, finally, by saying he could do more good if he stood guard in the hallway, in case any reporters came looking for me.

On the way home I was careful to keep my mind on my driving, all too aware of how exhausted I was. By the time I'd parked my truck in the garage and gone upstairs, it was nearly dark. My phone message light was blinking. Frannie, I thought. I wasn't ready to talk with her.

Frannie's voice on the tape sounded really concerned; she just wanted me to know that she knew, and would see me in the morning.

"Bless you, Frannie," I said.

After that I sank into my rocker, letting Sour-puss jump onto my lap. He settled in, and I took comfort in listening to the steady rumble of his purr and stroking his fur. I shook my head, squeezing back the tears.

Then I gave up, and just went ahead and cried.

FOURTEEN

My phone was ringing.

Struggling to bring myself out of my muddle-headed state, I got up and headed toward the bedroom to answer it, then realized I should play possum and let the answering machine take the call. Maybe it was a reporter. Or it might be Frannie—it would be just like her to decide she couldn't wait until tomorrow. Instead of Frannie's voice, I heard Joe's.

He said my name tentatively, sounding nervous and embarrassed, then stopped. I grabbed for the phone, worried he might hang up. Joe didn't like phones, and had even less tolerance for answering machines.

"Joe," I hollered over the last of the answering message. "Hang on. It's me, Emma. Don't hang up."

"That you, Emma?" There was an uncharacteristic squeak in his voice.

"Sorry about the machine," I said. Lord! I'd have to tell him what had happened today. I wasn't ready.

"Emma, about this trip. I called before, but that contraption of yours..."

"I'm sorry," I said again. "I...uh...had meant to be home sooner."

"Anyhow, I wanted to know where we're supposed to be on Wednesday. And when."

"I haven't had a chance to find out yet. I'll have to call you tomorrow."

I could fill him in tomorrow about what had happened with Rebecca.

"Trapper Creek, by golly," Joe said. "I hadn't known anyone was doing river runs up there. It's nice country, real pretty."

He wanted to talk about the trip, but I wasn't sure I'd be able to keep up a good front much longer.

"Like I said, I'll have to call you tomorrow," I told him. I didn't want to hurt his feelings, but as soon as I could, I ended the conversation.

I sat down at the kitchen table to think, trying to sort out all the pieces. Rebecca had said I took something that belonged to her grandmother, or at least that's what I thought she meant. The cradle, most likely. But she'd tried to tell me something else, I was certain of it. She must have known who the man with the hood pulled over his face was.

Then there was tomorrow to think about. Holmes wanted me to stick around. But Clara and her Pomo Indian friends were counting on help for that trip. I thought I could get myself together and go, but I wasn't sure I wanted to—not now.

I couldn't think. The room was hot and stuffy. I'd closed up the place this morning against the day's heat, and had been too out of it when I'd come home to notice anything.

I opened the windows, got out of my grubby clothes, and took a cold shower. It worked. I felt better.

It occurred to me that the shooting was probably on the late news, and I'd better see what they were saying. I went over and snapped on the television. The picture came up showing Rebecca's face. It looked like a snapshot, a photo that must have come out of someone's family album.

They had interview footage with the man from the cafe. At first he was talking about Rebecca, how long she'd worked there and how strangely she'd behaved the afternoon the dead baby was found. Then—good grief!—he started talking about me. He didn't know my name, of course, but he talked about how Rebecca had run away when I'd come in that first time. He said he'd told me that Rebecca was interested in the old Queen

Anne, and described it as "sort of like a haunted house." Then he began going on about *things* happening years ago with the people who lived there—the same salacious chop-licking that he'd gone through before. It bothered me even more this time.

The news announcer came back on. He recapped the finding of the baby and who the house had belonged to. A Damien Enterprises truck had been sighted near the old house, he said. A spokesperson for Damien Enterprises said it had not been assigned to the Victorian Villa project, but stolen from another construction site.

"While Fairville police decline to comment on a possible connection between the discovery of the infant's body and this afternoon's tragic death," he commented, "the investigation continues. Now, back to our reporter on the scene, Margaret Wheeler."

The screen showed a young woman standing in front of the Queen Anne. She began talking about the dead baby and the two "women of mystery." It took a minute to figure out who she meant by that—Rebecca and me.

"Restaurant owner Max Sutherland calls this a haunted house." She turned, gesturing toward the Queen Anne. "*Is* this house haunted?" The camera slowly zoomed in for a long look. ''Does the spirit of a long-dead baby linger here? And now, perhaps, the spirit of Rebecca Higgins?''

I turned off the television in disgust and headed for bed, where I tossed and turned long after I'd hoped to be asleep.

I WAS AWAKENED by the sound of a car pulling into Frannie's driveway.

Var-room...*var-room*...*VAR-ROOM*!

It had to be that damn Datsun Z of Whitaker's. He must have jiggered with the exhaust system somehow to give it that sound. Adolescent stuff.

I looked at my clock. Almost midnight.

After everything else that had gone wrong today, Frannie had gone out with *him*. It was bad enough that Whitaker was going to be more than a passing fancy, now the idiot had to come around and make noise right under my bedroom window.

I could hear their voices as they got out of the car. She was giggling. His voice sounded oddly different to me for a moment, until I realized he was doing John Wayne imitations. The phrase ''little lady'' was sprinkled liberally in the conversation. I could imagine him proffering his arm to Frannie, making a big show of escorting her up the walk. She never gets tired of the Prince Charming bit.

There was a brief silence. They must have been on her porch, and Frannie was likely going through her demure Doris Day hand-him-the-key routine. Frannie loves playacting; in some ways, I don't think she's ever really grown up.

The door opened, closed.

Silence.

But right away I heard the door open again, and then Whitaker's quick footsteps going back to his car. Frannie must have done the complete Doris Day innocent routine; she'd obviously given him the fast shuffle tonight. The car door slammed noisily and the engine revved. Maybe Whitaker hadn't expected to strike out. He was obviously doing *angry* for Frannie's benefit. He gave the engine a couple of extra loud var-rooms before he backed out and drove away.

I had to smile.

The situation wasn't too serious yet. Otherwise Whitaker would have left much, much later—and been very, very quiet about it.

FIFTEEN

I AWOKE TO bright sunshine and a cool, brisk breeze blowing through the apartment.

I'd decided to go on the river trip. Holmes shouldn't object, not if I checked in with him first, especially since I'd be safely out of the reach of reporters. I dressed quickly and went out on my porch to admire the day. Frannie was in the garden below, fussing around in the back flower bed.

"Emma!" she hallooed up at me. "I was just picking some flowers for the breakfast table. Come down and eat with me. I've fixed enough for both of us."

I was hungry enough for one of Frannie's breakfasts; I'd missed supper last night.

"We'll have croissants," Frannie called. "I took some out of the freezer." She fussed for a minute with the yellow daisies she'd picked. "I've been worried about you," she added.

Not worried enough to stay home last night, I thought, but a few moments later I was in Frannie's breakfast nook, watching as she heaped sausage and scrambled eggs onto my plate.

"What happened yesterday—that was just so terrible," Frannie said. "The poor woman. Gracious! And you right there. You might have been . . ." Her voice trailed off.

"I know," I told her.

We were both silent for a moment, then Frannie started bustling around and put another croissant on my plate.

"Emma, what in heaven's name were you doing at that cafe?"

I told her the whole story, starting with Rebecca following me the day I'd found the baby. Frannie clucked and sympathized and scolded me for not having told her about that—or the cradle. She was especially excited about what the initials *AD* might mean. Then she got to wondering how the cradle came to be under the porch.

"Somebody must have given it to Rebecca. Gracious! Why would anyone give an antique cradle to a woman like that?"

I was annoyed, feeling defensive of Rebecca, but all I said was that I had no idea. But Frannie caught my annoyance. "Here, have some marmalade for your croissant," she said, quickly getting off the subject. "This is some I made. It's got ginger and lemon rind in it."

She waited a moment before she spoke again.

"Goodness! Do you think Rebecca really was one of those hippies living there in that old Victorian house?"

"I suppose so," I said, adding that I'd been trying to figure out what might have happened so long ago.

"It's a real-life mystery, isn't it?" Frannie said, a note of delicious excitement in her voice.

"It's a mystery to me, all right."

"Oh, but we can be detectives. Let's talk it through and see what we can come up with."

"Okay," I said. "Let's go back to the sixties. Rebecca was living there. The upstairs room might have belonged to somebody else, but let's just say it was hers. And there are a bunch of other people living in the house."

"Because it's some sort of commune."

"Yes," I conceded.

"Then she has her baby."

"She has the baby, but apparently something happened to it, and she didn't know what. She'd seemed to think it was still alive. The man at the restaurant told me a psychic was filling her head with a bunch of nonsense. She was supposed to watch over the house, as if she might learn something about her baby."

"Oh, how strange. And how sad!"

"So, Rebecca has the baby, but then the baby is somehow gone. As near as I can gather, she didn't know it was dead. She must have been frantic trying to figure out where it was. So maybe about then something happened to her. She must have gone somewhere—most of her things weren't in the room, but she'd left some stuff behind. Where do you suppose she went?"

"You mean after she was home from the hospital, after the baby was born?"

"Yes, assuming she went to a hospital. She might have had the baby right there in the house, with a midwife."

"Oh! That's right, it was one of those communes." Frannie shook her head, scowling. "Hippies."

"Oh, come on, Frannie! Some of the people who lived in communes were all right—idealistic. Not all communes were bad, you know."

Frannie sniffed. "Drugs and all," she said.

She was probably right about that when it came to the people who lived at the Queen Anne. There'd been Nancy Teagarden's arrest, and Rebecca was certainly addle-brained enough to have done some messing around with hard drugs.

"Rebecca wasn't very stable. Maybe, after the baby came, she sort of went over the edge for a while."

"She could have been sent to a mental hospital."

"That would make sense. Except that she would have taken, at most, only a couple of changes of clothes. But Vince said there weren't any clothes in that upstairs room, just an old bathing suit."

"Who's Vince?" Frannie asked eagerly.

I'd be in real trouble if Frannie Edmundson, world-class matchmaker, ever decided to make a project out of me and Vince.

"Vince Valenti. He's with the Fairville police."

"And ... ?"

"And nothing. Vince did me a favor and told me what they found in the room, that's all. It was the kind of stuff people don't need every day— phonograph records, photographs, that kind of thing. There were some old newspapers strewn around, too."

"Old newspapers?"

"A copy of the *Fairville Reporter*, and some pages from a scandal sheet called the *Globe-Tattler*. There was a page torn from the *Reporter*."

I hadn't thought of it before, but Vince had copied only one side of that page. Something important might have been on the other side.

"What page was torn?" Frannie asked.

"The front page. I noticed it because it had a picture of the civil rights march on Washington."

I decided I'd pay a visit to the state library. They had a collection of back issues of all the newspapers in California. I told Frannie I wanted to check what was on the *Fairville Reporter* page that had been torn, then thanked her for the breakfast, and hurried home to grab my purse and close the windows.

I was double-timing down the stairs when I saw our next-door neighbor, Velma Patterson, lurking in the driveway. The woman is a gossip and a snoop. I didn't want to have to talk to her, or, more precisely, listen to what she had to say. I called out a cheery "Good morning!" and kept moving.

As I backed the truck down the drive, Velma still stood there, obviously determined to sidetrack me.

"Nice day," I said through the open truck window as I backed past her. "Going to be a little cooler, I think."

"Mrs. Chizzit," she called after me as I neared the street. "Your stove—is it working okay now?"

Whatever excuse for a conversation she'd dreamed up this time, it could wait until later. I hoped she'd take it up with Frannie so I'd be off the hook.

I managed to find a parking place near the Library and Courts Building, then hurried in and took the elevator up to the third floor. Before I went in to search for the old copy of the *Reporter*, I asked the librarian about back issues of the *Globe-Tattler*—not that I was very hopeful they'd have it.

"We have only California newspapers," the librarian said.

"I guess most libraries don't carry that kind of stuff."

"I can check for you, to see if I can find out if any one has it."

I thanked her, gave her my name and phone number, and headed for the microfilm stacks. I found the back files of the *Reporter*, and then the microfilm cannister for the last half of 1963—the civil rights march had been sometime that fall. I whizzed the issues through the viewer, stopping only long enough to look at each first page. When I'd found the issue I was looking for, I positioned the reverse side of the front page on the viewer, moving it to scan the columns and catch each headline.

Damien Enterprises Reorganized.

This had to be it.

It was a strange article. P.J. Damien had called a press conference to announce a "restructuring of assets." Though the article said exactly where and when the press conference had been held, there was no mention of what assets were involved, or exactly how the Damien organization had changed. Instead, starting with the third paragraph, there was nothing but descriptions of the several Damien projects then under way in or near Fairville. That was all, except for a final, brief mention that the new Mrs. Damien—Belle—was vacationing in Europe.

I sat back and stared at the fuzzy words on the screen.

There had to be some way this made sense. The headline said *reorganization*; the story said *restructuring of assets*. Those words could mean anything or nothing. Maybe old P.J. had decided to shuffle his pots of money around, or name new officers in his corporation for tax reasons. That wasn't the kind of stuff a developer would want made public. Yet he'd called a press conference, and the local newspaper, which must have been practically in his hip pocket, had written a non-story.

Small-town newspapers won't do anything to offend a major advertiser. Old P.J. must have wanted some kind of story in print, even if they were unwilling to print what he'd decided to announce. I suppose the *Reporter* had run this vague article, which wasn't any kind of story at all, with the idea that they couldn't afford to ignore the press conference.

But why would P.J. have called a press conference?

He might have been mad at the local planning commission, or some such thing. But there were those old pages of the *Globe-Tattler* out in the hallway. If the *Tattler* had carried the story, then whatever old P.J. had announced at that press conference must have had some juicy scandal behind it.

I quickly copied the *Reporter* article, though I thought it had no value except to indicate there had to be something in the *Tattler*, and hurried to a pay phone. I wasn't going to give Holmes another chance to say that I'd failed to report significant information.

Holmes listened to what I had to say, but played the same old cold-fish game with me. I kept trying, hoping to elicit some kind of response from him. I read him the entire article and explained how I thought the back issue of the *Tattler* might be important.

The police were more likely to be able to get hold of a back issue of the *Tattler* than I was, and I was darn curious to know what might be in it. I pointed out to Holmes that Damien Enterprises might be somehow involved in this whole mess, which is exactly what I'd come to believe. He was courteous, and absolutely uncommunicative. I gave up, and told him that I would be away for one day on the river trip, which seemed to be all right with him. After I hung up, I dialed the Fairville police again and asked for Vince.

He was obviously delighted to hear from me, although I had to sit through a scolding for not letting him drive me back to Sacramento.

"You shouldn't have gone by yourself. You should have let me take you. Jeez—what if something happened to you?"

"I was just fine, Vince."

"Aw...you need someone to take care of you."

"Vince, I called to tell you that I went down to the library and looked at the other side of that page from the *Fairville Reporter*. There was an article there about Damien Enterprises."

"Yeah," he said, sounding abashed. "Holmes made me go back to the newspaper office and get the other side of the page."

"Holmes sure plays things close to the vest. I just called to read the article to him. He didn't even say he already had it."

"Holmes is going by the rule book whole hog. He won't talk to nobody."

"I also told him I thought there might be something in the *Globe-Tattler*."

"He kept quiet about that, too, huh?"

"Yes, he did."

"He won't tell nothing. But he got the same idea and went and called the *Tattler* office. He had a heck of a time getting ahold of anybody who would do anything for him. Jeez! You should have heard him on the phone, talking like he was the Emperor of Everywhere."

Vince launched into such a good imitation of Holmes that I had to laugh. Laughing was a mistake. It encouraged him to start doing the imitation all over again.

"'Holmes, here,'" Vince said, making his voice even more officious. " 'Fairville Police, Fairville, California.' "

I told him to stop before Holmes heard him.

"By the way, Vince, what was the date on that old issue of the *Tattler*?"

"First week in December 1963, I think. You want me to check?"

"No, that's close enough."

"You want to know something else? Holmes put in a call to Belle Damien. He's having fits—she hasn't called him back."

"Has anything else turned up?"

"Not really. Oh. Yeah. That guy was trying to do something to Rebecca's car before you got there."

"What kind of something?"

"Well, over by the front wheel on the driver's side was a painter's drop cloth, all neatly folded up on the ground. When you chased Rebecca out of that kitchen, he must have been just finishing up what he did."

"What did he do?"

"We looked under the car. He sliced the brake line on the left front wheel, but not quite all the way through. We almost missed it, but there was a drop of brake fluid sitting on the line where it was cut. The way the guys here figure it, what he did made it so her brakes would work okay at first. She'd get out of the parking lot and not notice, but the first time she really tromped on the brakes, the car would lurch to one side, and then the brakes would give out altogether."

I was silent, thinking.

"The guys down at the garage said the Karmann Ghia was one of those older models," Vince added. "No dual brake system. He planned it. He knew what he was doing. She'd be out in the traffic, and . . . ker-blooey!"

"Premeditated," I said.

"Yeah. He'd set his sights on her long before you showed up there."

SIXTEEN

THE PHONE CALL TO Vince had turned out to be a good idea, except that now I was having trouble getting disentangled from him.

"I'm awful worried," he said. "This guy knows you got a look at his face."

"Not much of a look."

"You might be in danger."

I reminded him that Holmes was keeping quiet about who I was.

"That don't matter. How about that sign on your truck door? It says A-1 Salvage."

"But I parked down the street. I don't think he would have known that was my truck."

"This guy must have been real antsy while he was working on Rebecca's car. You know, checking around all the time to see if anybody was coming. He might have seen you get out of your truck. And that sign's got your phone number."

"Vince, there's no area code with it."

Suppose, I thought, the man remembered both the sign and the phone number. What would he do? Even if he checked telephone directories outside the Fairville area, I wasn't listed as A-1 Salvage.

I told Vince that.

"Aw . . . he might find a way. You need protection. Like maybe I ought to come around and check on you sometimes. Suppose he checked business licenses for the towns around? Sure. He could do that. What if he checked in Sacramento and found you?"

"That's pretty farfetched, Vince." The thought actually made me a little uneasy—not that I was going to say so.

"I want you to be safe," Vince said with dogged determination.

I didn't like the implications. He was fishing for an excuse to hang around.

"Look," I told him, "I'll take the sign off the door of my truck. It's magnetic. I can peel it right off."

"Aw, Emma, he could find you anyways."

Vince had an idea in his head and wasn't about to be discouraged. He'd come over to Sacramento, he said, park his car nearby, watch over me.

"Even at night. I've slept in my car before. Plenty of times."

"No way," I told him. "Absolutely not."

I had to think of something to keep Old Lonely off my back.

"I'll tell you what," I said in desperation. "I'll give you Frannie Edmundson's phone number—she lives in that big house in front of my place—and if you call to check on me, and don't get an answer, you can call her to make sure I'm okay."

He bought the idea, reluctantly. I didn't like it much either, but at least it would keep him at a distance.

After I finally got off the phone with Vince, I made two more calls. One was to Judy to get the details of the next day's trip; the other to Joe to set things up with him. Then I headed home.

Frannie must have been watching for me. The minute I pulled into the driveway she came hurrying out the side door of her house. She positioned herself in front of me, hands on hips, sparks flying from her eyes.

"Emma Chizzit, how could you! How *dare* you!"

What was this all about? I got out of the truck warily.

"That was a despicable thing to do! Spying on Belle, sneaking around. Shame on you!" She was in front of me now, standing on tiptoe and shaking a finger right in my face.

"Wait a minute," I said, wondering if Belle had told Frannie about my visit. But that would turn all my notions about Belle upside down. I'd been certain she wouldn't mention my visit to anyone, let alone Frannie.

"How could you possibly *do* it?" Frannie wailed, switching abruptly from anger to plaintive disappointment.

"Do what?"

"Send someone to spy on Belle, that's what. Don't deny it—you sent that Vince Valenti off to do your dirty work."

That had me puzzled for a minute, until I remembered that I'd asked Vince to see what he could find out about the man Belle had been talking to at the shopping center. And I'd given Vince Frannie's phone number.

"Vince just called," Frannie went on. "I don't like it one bit, your thinking that Belle—after she gave you that job! For goodness' sake, Emma, what's Belle going to think of me now?"

"Frannie," I said, "I won't tell her, if you won't."

"Emma!"

"Let's stop and look at this for a minute, Frannie. I didn't ask Vince to find out something about Belle, just about someone I saw her talking to."

"Same thing," Frannie sniffed.

"Okay," I said. "You're right ... sort of."

She looked at me reproachfully.

"With all that's happened the last couple of days, I didn't want to leave out any possibilities for finding out what's going on. I just wanted to find out who Belle was talking to, that's all. He didn't look like part of the crowd that was there that day."

"Well, it doesn't seem right to me."

"I'm sorry if I hurt your feelings, Frannie."

"You could have told me what you were doing." She was beginning to relent. "You know I worry about you."

"Okay, Frannie. I'll tell you everything that happens from now on. I promise."

Of course, the interview with Belle didn't come under the category of *from now on*.

"Anyway," Frannie said, "your friend Vince Valenti really didn't have much to report."

All Vince had managed to learn, apparently, was that the man wasn't part of the security force hired for the shopping center party. Vince thought he might be a private investigator, and would check for concealed-weapons licenses.

"He said those licenses have photos," Frannie said, "and he'll copy any that match your description."

I thanked Frannie and apologized again for hurting her feelings. At the same time I was already regretting my promise to tell her everything. I didn't want to worry her.

I was about to put my truck in the garage when Velma Patterson came trotting out.

"I saw that workman at your apartment yesterday," she said. "I guess you left your door unlocked." She looked at me reproachfully. "You always leave your door unlocked."

"Someone went inside my place?"

"Yes. I thought it rather odd, so I made a point of talking to him when he came out. He said he was sent to repair your stove."

"I didn't send for anyone."

"And he wasn't dressed like a repairman, exactly. I mean he didn't have a uniform on."

"Oh?"

"That's why I wanted to talk to you. It looked all right to me at first, since he drove up a truck that looked like it belonged to some company—it was painted red and gray. But he was almost, well, furtive. And he was wearing a sweatshirt—in this hot weather, can you imagine?—a sweatshirt with the hood pulled up around his face.''

SEVENTEEN

I BOUNDED UP MY STAIRS, two at a time, not even stopping to consider that whatever the man in the sweatshirt had done in my place was done yesterday. Frannie came puffing right behind me to the top of the stairs as soon as I'd flung open the door.

"That smell!" Frannie exclaimed.

Gas. The apartment was filled with it.

I hurried inside to open the windows, then dashed out again.

Frannie and Velma Patterson were in a huddle at the bottom of the stairs.

"I'll call the utility company," Velma volunteered.

"Fine," I said.

"Don't go back in there, Emma," Frannie said. "Let the gas company people find the leak."

"Can I use your phone?" I asked her.

"What are you going to do?"

"Call the Fairville Police."

I talked with Holmes and explained what had happened. He asked a few questions, then said he'd get in touch with the Sacramento police;

they'd send an officer around to check things out and take statements. By then, Velma was tapping on Frannie's side door to let us know the men from the utility company were arriving.

I followed them up to my apartment, which had fairly well aired out by then. One went around to turn off the outside valve while the other went in.

"Here's your trouble, lady," he said after a few moments. "The pilot on your stove was out and one of the burners was turned part way on."

I couldn't figure it out. The man posing as a workman had been at my place yesterday, and I'd had the windows closed all day, so my place should have been filled with gas when I came home. And if the man in the sweatshirt had been here yesterday, he must have come straight to Sacramento after he'd shot Rebecca—with no time to fool around finding me through business licenses or phone directories.

So he'd already known where I lived.

Frannie and I sat in her breakfast nook, trying to decide on some plausible explanation. In the meantime, the Sacramento police had come and taken our statements. They were now going up and down the street to find out if any neighbors had seen the man in the sweatshirt.

"Emma, this is just terrible. I'm so worried about you."

"I'm a little worried about me, too," I admitted.

"What if he comes back?"

I'd been thinking about that. I had planned to pick up Joe first thing in the morning for the river trip. Now it seemed like a better idea to see if I could spend the night with Judy and Charlie Moore, and tell Joe to come over on his own. I told Frannie that's what I'd do.

We were still talking about it when Vince phoned. He'd just found out what had happened and was falling all over himself to come over and protect me. I told him I'd be staying with friends, explaining I'd be safe for that night and the next day. I finally managed to get him calmed down and off the phone.

"But what about after the trip is over?" Frannie asked.

"I'll just have to be like Scarlett O'Hara, and worry about that tomorrow."

I'd gone back up to my place, phoned both Judy and Joe, and was busy getting my things together for the river trip when the phone rang. I decided to be smart and play possum. It was Vince again, wishing he hadn't missed me. He'd rather be watching out for me, he said, but would do the next best thing—take tomorrow off to see what he could learn about Belle and what she was up to. He'd go to the Damien mansion early and follow her through the day.

"Maybe you won't let me protect you, but I'll be on the job. I'm gonna find out something. We got to solve this case."

It sounded like a wild-goose chase to me, but he was so terribly earnest and anxious that I was touched.

Another phone call came in just before I left, and I decided to let the tape recorder take that one, too. It was the woman from the state library. None of the public libraries kept files of the *Tattler*, she said, but a retired journalism professor who'd made a study of this sort of thing had a collection that might include it. I grabbed for a paper and pencil as she gave his name and phone number.

Neal Stringer. The phone number was in the San Jose area. I dialed it right away and a man answered.

"Professor Stringer?"

"Yes."

I told him my name and what I wanted.

"The *Globe-Tattler*? Marvelous rag. I used it all the time in my class on ethics in journalism. Are you a journalism student?"

"Not exactly. I need to know what's in one of the back issues because I'm trying to...um...track down someone."

"Sounds interesting. I used to use those rags myself a bit—did some investigative reporting for a while after I retired. You doing a little reporting, writing a book maybe?"

"No. Just trying to get some background so I can locate someone. Do you have the *Tattlers* as far back as 1963?"

"I most certainly do. Began my collection in 1960. Started teaching the ethics class in, let's see, I think the following year."

"Do you have the first week in December 1963?"

"Of course. Say, who are you trying to locate?"

"I'm kind of in a hurry. Can you check and see if you have the first week in December?"

"That was a good year. Provocative material, a great commentary on—"

"I'm sorry to be so brusque, but could you possibly copy the first issue for December 1963 and send it to me? I'll mail you a check to cover the cost and your trouble.''

I was getting more edgy all the time, wanting to clear out of my place. The man was exasperatingly chatty, but finally agreed to copy the issue and send it by express mail so I'd get it right away.

I scribbled a check and put it in an envelope addressed to him, gathered up my things, and set a big dish of dry catfood on the porch for Sourpuss. On my way out of town, I mailed the letter at the main post office.

I SET OUT for Trapper Creek, heading west on the freeway. I was still tense, looking at each car that passed me, constantly scanning the rearview mirror.

I made a deliberate effort to relax, stretching as I drove, rotating my shoulders and wiggling my head to take the tension out of my muscles. I turned north off the freeway, willing myself to think about tomorrow and speculate about the trip. As I took the winding road that led up through Madrone Valley, I at last began to worry less.

This was attractive countryside, dotted with huge valley oaks, planted mostly with hayfields and orchards. The slope was gentle, but the valley was steadily narrowing, the hills closing in on either side. There were rank upon rank of ridges clothed in chaparral and scrub oak, with their promise of steep canyons and rushing streams. In the hills north of San Francisco there are few trappings of civilization, except in the valleys and along the highways. The dry steep hills are wilderness terrain. Deer and jackrabbits abound, and there are a few coyotes and mountain lions. Farther north, the wilderness areas are even larger. It's empty country, empty enough so that those crazy legends about Bigfoot don't seem so farfetched after all.

As I neared the top end of the valley, I was surprised by the sight of a huge gash in a hill alongside the road ahead. When I got closer I saw a billboard proclaiming *Hi Stakes Bingo*! and a plastic banner: *Jackpot To-nite = $10,000*. There was a monstrous new building with an even more monstrous parking lot. The hillside had been cruelly cut to make enough level ground for this establishment, the raw embankment already eroding and etched with deep gullies.

Just up the road was the Madrone *rancheria*, a motley collection of cinder block houses with scrubby yards, derelict vehicles, tar paper sheds, and abandoned-looking chicken coops. But there was a big dish antenna, new-looking, and some fancy pickup trucks, loaded with chrome and special equipment, parked by several of the houses.

Following the instructions Judy had given me, I turned left on Madrone Avenue, followed it for a distance of about a city block, and turned left again where it dead-ended at Oak Flat Road. I soon found a cluster of mail boxes, one labeled Moore. I turned right to cross a rickety bridge over a dry creek bed. Here was the Moores' driveway, a half mile of narrow dirt track winding steeply up a small hill. Just over the brow of the hill was a little house and a big barn with a large bare area in front of it, all overlooking a small valley.

I parked in front of the barn and was getting my sleeping bag out of the truck when Judy came out of the house to greet me, a little girl of about three trailing behind her. Judy surprised me with a hug, her affection so eager it almost bordered on anxiety. Then she introduced her daughter, Marie. I knelt down and got busy trying to make friends with little Marie.

"Here's Charlie," Judy said.

I looked up, eager to meet him. "Indian Charlie" was handsome, a slender man in his late thirties with pale, clear skin, striking blue eyes, and a shock of dark brown hair.

He smoothed his hair back with a nervous gesture and shook hands with me.

"Glad you could make it," he said, favoring me with a boyish grin, "and double-glad you could be here tonight."

He reached for my sleeping bag and started toward the house. As Judy and I followed, I noticed he was limping. As soon as my belongings were inside the front door, Charlie said we'd have to go back outside and put my truck in the barn.

"What happened to your leg?" I asked as we went out together to move my truck.

"I was helping Judy and Clara set up for the show at the shopping center, and a ladder gave out under me." He grinned wryly. "A very tall ladder."

"Too bad," I said. "Looks like a nasty sprain."

"Nasty might be exactly the right word for it."

Marie had clambered into my truck. She sat behind the wheel, pretending to steer. Charlie went to open the barn door, and I took Marie into my lap.

"You can drive the truck into the barn," I told her as I started the motor. We pulled into the barn, four hands on the steering wheel. Then I got the rest of my belongings, took Marie in my arms, and Charlie and I started toward the house.

I'd noticed a lot of rafting equipment in the barn, a station wagon, and a mud-spattered Bronco. Odd, I thought, that they didn't just park in the open space out front. I wondered why Charlie had gone to the trouble of having me put my truck in the barn, and asked him.

He gestured at Marie. "I'll tell you later," he said.

EIGHTEEN

I HAD TO WAIT for Marie's bedtime to ask about this business of keeping vehicles hidden in the barn. In the meantime, all through supper, I made conversation.

"Clara told me about Reliance Enterprises," I said to Judy. "She explained that you and Charlie started it, after you came back to the *rancheria*."

Judy responded eagerly, launching into the story of how she'd met Charlie. After she'd finished school, she told me, she'd become more and more discouraged about conditions at the *rancheria*.

"I wanted to separate myself from my background, get a long ways away. I went to Vancouver, but living there wasn't working out for me. I missed home and I felt terribly guilty, just walking out on all the problems like that. Then I met Charlie."

"You made a big impression on me," Charlie said. "You just about knocked my socks off."

Judy grinned and blushed.

"Judy is exactly the right kind of woman for me," Charlie said, taking up the story. "I was married before, to a woman who thought money was the most important thing in the world. She had a lot of it, too, and we spent money... cars, parties, clothes, jetting around. I got sick of it. It was all so useless." He shook his head sadly. "It bothers me even more now, the way we spent that money."

Judy was watching him, her eyes aglow.

"Money is to accomplish things with, to make the world a better place," Charlie said.

"Amen," I added.

"My family had a little money, too," Charlie said. "But they weren't like that. They were nice people. Remember, Judy, how I used to talk about my grandmother from Toronto? She'd come to see us when I was a kid, Emma, and I always loved her visits. She didn't bring presents. She gave me her time and attention—taught me things, took me places. She showed me how some people have to live, because I'd never been around people who didn't have enough money. She really was concerned about helping people. She cared about the environment, too. I still remember our trip down the Olympic peninsula, my first experience in a real wilderness."

"Maybe that's how you got started on river rafting," I said, hoping to steer the conversation back to what was going on now.

"It could be," he said thoughtfully.

"Charlie had been running rivers for a few years when I met him," Judy said. "He was looking for a river that hadn't been commercialized yet, to start his own business."

"Trapper Creek was just a natural choice," Charlie said. "For both of us."

"And then, when you saw how things were here," I prompted, "you started Reliance Enterprises."

"Right," Judy said.

Charlie glanced at his watch. "Hey, Marie, time for you to be getting to bed." He scooped up the little girl and gave her a hug. "It's Daddy's turn to read you a story tonight."

While he was busy with Marie, Judy and I cleared the table and washed the dishes. When Charlie came back out to join us at the supper table for a second cup of coffee, I asked the Moores why they were keeping their vehicles and my truck buttoned up inside the barn.

"We don't want anybody to be able to tell who is here," Judy said quickly.

"But why?"

Judy glanced nervously toward Charlie.

"We've had a few problems," he said. "It's begun to look as if someone doesn't like us."

"They don't like what we're doing," Judy added.

"They?"

"Developers, who else?" she said vehemently.

"We can't say that for sure," Charlie said.

"Maybe you can't, but I can! We've stood for just about enough from—"

I interrupted. "Stood for just about enough of what?"

"So-called accidents," Judy said, her voice tightening, going shrill. "You can't call what happened this afternoon an accident, Charlie. You could have been—" She broke off, close to crying. Charlie put an arm around her shoulders.

"What's happened?" I asked.

Charlie explained. His fall from the ladder had been no accident; he'd taken a good look later and discovered someone had tampered with it. Before that, a potentially lethal short circuit had turned up in a power tool he was about to use—more sabotage.

"All very subtle," Judy said bitterly. "Everyone knows how careless Indians are about keeping equipment in good repair."

"Come on, Judy," Charlie said. "That's got nothing to do with it."

"Well, they're trying to stop us, keep us powerless, make us into... into nothing."

"They. You mean developers."

"Who else? They're really threatened by Reliance Enterprises."

"Apparently, some developers have plans for the area," Charlie explained.

"They don't want us to keep our land," Judy added. "They don't want us to have anything to pass on to our children."

Charlie looked over at me.

"We've just found out—Marie is going to have a little brother or sister."

"Congratulations," I said, and then realized how foolish it sounded under the circumstances. Something serious had to have happened, I thought. Newly pregnant women can get upset easily, but even considering that, she was far too upset to be worried just over the two incidents they'd told me about.

"I only hope that baby isn't born an orphan," Judy said. "Charlie, go ahead and tell her about this afternoon."

"Somebody tried to run me off the road. I was coming down from the hills, from the other direction than the way you came in, Emma. There's a spot there where the road is steep and narrow, winding down into the canyon from the ridge. I'd seen him—the guy who tried to run me off the road—driving up the hill a few minutes earlier. He must have been looking for me, and turned around and come back. Anyhow, he came right up behind me. Then, at a turn, he tried to move alongside, get between me and the uphill embankment. I'd swear he planned to ram me and push me right over the edge.''

"What happened?"

"I accelerated, swerved to the right, and skidded around the turn."

"And you're sure he did it on purpose."

"Absolutely," Charlie said.

"And it wasn't just anybody," Judy added. "It was somebody driving a Damien truck."

I almost dropped my coffee cup.

Impossible, I thought—not the same man. How could he have gotten here before I did? No, this was something separate, it had to be. But, still, he'd known right where to find me after he shot Rebecca.

I asked Charlie if he'd gotten a look at the man driving the truck.

"Not really. But I think he was wearing dark glasses. And he looked strange, like he had something over his hair."

I might have known. For now, I decided not to say anything about Rebecca's death and the attempt on my own life.

"I never trusted Belle Damien from the start," Judy said. "I wasn't fooled for a minute with all this business about letting us sell baskets at her new shopping center. That was just a cover-up, a way to pretend she wanted to help us. We were supposed to think she's our friend, so we won't catch on to what she wants to do around here."

"Judy," Charlie said, "we've got reason to think developers are after this land, but no reason to suspect Belle Damien more than any of the others."

His voice was more impatient than his words, which I found curious. It almost seemed as if he were defending Belle.

"Why not suspect her?" Judy said. "Put all the others together, and you still wouldn't have half the land and the money that Belle Damien has."

"She couldn't be that bad."

"Charlie has a point," I said. "She has a lot more to lose than some fly-by-night operator with no reputation or money, or someone from New

York, or from out of the country, who just plain doesn't care."

But, I thought to myself, an uncaring entrepreneur from some distant place wasn't likely to know the country or the local people well enough to resort to dirty tricks. My logic was falling to pieces, even while I was trying to assemble it.

"There's something else, too," Charlie said. "Belle wouldn't be stupid enough to send a henchman in one of her own trucks."

"That's right," I said.

In a moment I was struck with the thought that Belle could be smart enough to do just exactly that. But that theory crumbled right away, too. I couldn't believe Belle capable of planning murder.

NINETEEN

THAT NIGHT I SPENT sleepless hours thinking about the man in the sweatshirt. He might somehow have known yesterday that I was going to come up here, but it seemed far likelier that he had another reason, not connected to me or Rebecca, to be going after Charlie.

Nonetheless, by morning I'd decided to check with Frannie before we left on the trip. By this time I was ready to worry about anything, and wanted to make sure everything at home was all right.

As soon as we finished eating, I asked the Moores if I could use their phone. I was disappointed to be greeted only by the recorded message on Frannie's answering machine. That disturbed me for a minute, but then I thought to check my answering machine. I dialed my number, then punched the code to see if she'd left a message.

"Hel-lo," the mechanical voice said. "You have one message."

I waited.

"Emma?" Frannie's voice. "I know you're not home. I thought you might call, and I wanted you to know I'm all right, in case you do. I'm just too uneasy to stay home. Melissa's going to come get me and we'll spend the day shopping over by Fairville. I hope you have a nice trip, and ... um ... toodle-oo! Bye-bye now."

I left some money by the phone and began collecting my belongings. The day promised to be a busy one. Joe would be showing up soon, and Charlie's helper Ed Silva and his wife Rosie. Rosie was Judy's aunt, the one who was a basket maker. Judy and Rosie would spend the morning at the *Palladium* shopping center, keeping an appointment with the editor of a regional arts magazine.

"Belle Damien set it up," Judy announced, her distaste for Belle obvious.

The Silvas were the first to arrive, pulling into the yard in an old Power Wagon. Ed Silva was a man close to my age. He was small, narrow-shouldered, and wiry, thin in the face and rather sad-looking. He didn't look Indian to me—Portuguese, maybe. Charlie had been waiting impatiently for Ed, and hurried out the minute he spotted his truck; the two of them got busy haul-

ing rafting equipment out of the barn and loading it into the Power Wagon.

Rosie came bustling into the kitchen, a rotund,
middle-aged woman with a round race, broad
cheekbones, and a very nice smile.

"Those are beautiful baskets you make," I told
Rosie as soon as we were introduced. "It seems a
shame to part with them."

"I like making baskets," she told me. She
shrugged, as if to make light of the countless hours
I knew had to be spent on each one. "I can always make more."

Outside, I could see Joe arriving in his battered
Volkswagen bug. Charlie had backed his Bronco
out of the barn by then, and was busy directing
Joe to park inside.

Charlie departed to collect the New York reporter and his VIP guest from the Bureau of Indian Affairs. Before long, Joe, Ed, and I were
trundling up the road with the rafting equipment
in the old Power Wagon. I'd had the impression
Ed was assigned to do some explaining about what
Joe and I were to do on the trip, but he wasn't
much of a talker. We drove in silence for a while,
winding our way through the last of the hayfields
and pasture land at the upper tip of the valley and
toward the hilly country beyond.

"When I drove in yesterday," I said, just to be making conversation, "I saw that big new bingo establishment."

Ed rolled down the window. "Bingo people!" he said, and spat.

"It's hard to believe," I went on, "that folks would drive all the way out here just to—"

"You oughta see it nights and weekends," Ed said in disgust. "Cars, buses—damn parking lot's full of 'em." He spat again, emphatically, and rolled up the window. "A man can't even drive down the road in peace."

Ed clearly had his reasons for helping Charlie.

We wound our way up out of the valley, negotiating a steep set of curves, one of which must have been where Charlie had almost been forced over the edge. Then we turned off onto a narrow stretch of rutted road along the spine of a high, scrub-covered ridge. Next came a steep and tricky descent, for which Ed had to put the truck into four-wheel drive. I was grateful for the circumstances—no Damien pickup was going to make it down this hill.

We drove out onto a grassy flat studded with huge oaks. I caught my first sight of Trapper Creek, making a big horseshoe bend around three sides of the flat. Ed bumped across a rocky beach to the water's edge. The three of us got busy right away, moving the rafts and the inflating equipment out of the Power Wagon. We soon had the rafts ready and loaded with oars, lunch makings, and life vests for everybody.

"How's this going to work?" I asked Ed. "Who goes in which boat?"

"Charlie takes the big shots. He goes out first, then you two." He gave me a snaggletoothed grin. "I come along last, with the lunch."

"Suits me fine," I said, grateful that Ed would be following us on the river. "But I'm not sure you need me and Joe."

"Charlie's idea. He likes plenty of people, good talkers."

I supposed Charlie had the right idea. The trip would look less impressive with only he and Ed to cater to the VIPs, and Ed certainly wasn't much of a conversationalist. I didn't mind having been recruited mainly as a socializer, since I usually have to save carefully to go on a trip like this. One thing made me uneasy. While I've had a fair amount of experience with canoes, inflatables are another story.

"These two-man rafts," I said. "I haven't ever paddled one."

Ed grinned again, but said nothing. I knew he wouldn't mind seeing us "good talkers" take a spill—as long as the lunch was in his boat.

"Looks like we've got some time, Emma," Joe said. "Maybe we ought to try it out a bit."

I was glad for a chance to practice, and to have a private conversation with Joe. We put on our life jackets and paddled upstream, careful to stay in the quiet water near shore. The rushing water tumbling over boulders in midstream made a fair amount of noise, and it wasn't long before we were able to talk with no worries about being overheard.

I filled Joe in on what had been happening, and we began to speculate about the man in the sweatshirt.

"Most of the things he's done," I said, "have been planned to look like accidents—except for shooting Rebecca, of course."

"Clever fellow."

"He's gone after both Rebecca and Charlie," I said, "which doesn't make any sense at all to me. But the rest of what he's done follows a pattern. He would have arranged an accident for Rebecca if I hadn't chased her out of that cafe. And he tried to arrange an accident for me."

"I've been thinking," Joe said, "about how it could have happened that there wasn't any gas accumulated in your place at first."

"That's been bothering me. How could he have done it? He made his visit. Then I came home, but didn't open the windows for hours. It wasn't until the next day that the gas went on, or maybe during the night. I wouldn't have noticed with all the windows open and the breeze blowing through."

"When your neighbor saw him at your apartment, I think he was there to do two things," Joe explained. "He went inside and turned on the burner, but he also must have gone around back and turned off the main valve. That way he could come back anytime to start the gas going into your apartment."

"Right! He could just stroll up the alley. One quick twist of the wrist, and...."

"Clever fellow," Joe said again.

We were both silent, thinking.

"He may be clever," I said after a while, "but I think he's an amateur."

"How so?"

"All of his ideas have been ingenious, and pretty much on the mechanical side, but he's failed repeatedly. I don't know what professional hired killers do, but it seems to me they'd have to develop a pretty good batting average or go out of business.''

I took little comfort from that. The man was an amateur and, by now, probably a very frustrated one. When he was presented with the unexpected, he'd panicked and shot Rebecca, when he could as easily have stayed out of sight to wait for another opportunity. I didn't like it. We were dealing with a frustrated, panic-prone individual.

Joe pointed to a trail of dust on the opposite hillside. The Bronco was winding down the steep road to the flat. We paddled back and beached our raft as the Bronco came to a stop just above the beach; Charlie and one VIP got out. The man was wearing brand new clothes, with the store wrinkles still in, and looking as if they came from some fancy outdoor equipment place. This dude was a genuine tenderfoot.

Charlie started in right away with introductions.

''Elmer, this is my associate, Ed Silva. He's one of the most knowledgeable boatmen in these parts.'' Ed looked ill at ease, but Charlie was laying it on like an old pro. ''Ed, this is Elmer Rodriguez of the Bureau of Indian Affairs. And,'' Charlie went on, turning to Joe and me, ''here are today's helpers, Joe Simpson and Emma Chizzit. They've both been around the water a long time."

I squared my shoulders, trying to look as robust and competent as possible.

"Jesse Halliday from New York couldn't make it," Charlie said, offering no explanation.

Rodriguez didn't offer much conversation to go along with his limp handshake. Instead, he kept glancing over toward the water. It didn't take long to catch on that he was more than a little apprehensive about this trip.

Charlie had caught it, too. "Okay," he proclaimed loudly, "let's get going!" He'd already gotten into his lifejacket, and gestured at Ed to put his on. At the same time he was moving quickly to get Rodriguez buckled good and tight into his vest.

"Let's round 'em up," Charlie shouted, Wagonmaster style, the minute he had the life jacket on Rodriguez. "Head 'em up, and moo-oove 'em out!"

A minute later we had all three rafts in the river.

I sat in the back, my paddle idle in my hands, and watched the current as we drifted downstream toward the first small set of rapids. It was hardly more than a riffle, going around a gentle bend in the stream. Up ahead, Charlie was heading into it, sliding smoothly to cut across the curve. *Cut your C's, go down the center of the V's*—right out of the rule book. Joe, sitting upright and motionless in the front of our raft, was studying Charlie's every move. I could see Rodriguez hanging tightly onto the sides of the raft. Our tenderfoot was obviously experiencing a serious episode of white-knuckle syndrome.

We followed Charlie and Ed, taking the riffle easily, then we were on smooth water again. I split my attention between the water and the scenery. The canyon sides were alternately narrowing and spreading out, bringing swifter current and then slower going. I had time to study the landscape and the clear sky, empty of any evidence of human life except a thin, far-off contrail.

We stopped once, at mid-morning, mostly to let everybody take a hike in the bushes. Rodriguez was trailing behind Charlie as the two of them came back, so Charlie took the chance to tell Joe and me that the New York reporter had changed his mind at the last minute and was working on another story. Charlie didn't seem the least disappointed.

"He's assured me he'll do a story on Trapper Creek, sooner or later," Charlie said. "You two can have another trip if you're up to it. Also, I need to tell you, there's a couple of places to watch out for later today." He glanced over his shoulder. Rodriguez was quickly approaching. "Check with Ed if you get the chance. We'll be getting to some interesting spots."

Rodriguez was beside us, looking decidedly uncomfortable. Ed spoke up then, suddenly possessed by an uncharacteristic talkativeness. He turned his attention to Rodriguez, favoring him with a big grin, and began reciting with enthusiasm the names of the rapids we'd be encountering.

"Mad Mike's Downfall, the Mario Andretti run, Widowmaker—good stuff coming up."

Charlie was quick to cut in, starting a lively explanation about geologic formations in the canyon walls. While Charlie was going on about million-year-old seabeds, Ed caught my eye for an instant, then gazed into the distance, his face a mask of perfect innocence. He'd hear about this from Charlie later, of course. And I knew he wouldn't mind the chewing out in the least.

By the time we reached our lunch stop, the day had become downright hot. I was glad for the cool water that soaked my tennis shoes as we beached and unloaded the rafts. The canyon had opened out here, the stream moving more slowly, with tree-shaded flats on either side of the river. Ours, on the outer side of a bend, was the larger. On the hillside opposite was the first road I'd seen since we started down the river, a narrow dirt track zigzagging down to the other beach.

Charlie pulled Rodriguez off into a conversation right away, not giving Ed another chance at him. Joe and I set to work helping Ed get out the lunch fixings, and I listened with interest to the bits of Charlie's pitch I could manage to overhear. He was eagerly citing numbers of people on various river trips and using phrases like *economic opportunities* and *creative enterprise*. It was a first-class presentation.

Charlie knew how to put on a class act in the lunch department, too. He'd supplied a colorful checked tablecloth and cloth napkins. I busied myself cutting up the crusty French bread, while Ed brought out delicatessen-sliced roast beef and prosciutto ham, Greek olives, red bell pepper strips, and imported mustard.

The lunch made a hit with Rodriguez, although Charlie did more talking than eating. Joe and Ed launched into the food with gusto. It was a success with me, too, although I could have done with a cup of coffee.

Afterward I was feeling pleasantly relaxed. Charlie insisted on repacking the lunch equipment. I was about ready to take a snooze, but was unwilling, however, to leave poor Rodriguez to Ed's tender mercies, and ambled over to the shade of a big cottonwood where he'd settled himself.

"Beautiful scenery," I said, trying to sound enthusiastic about talking to him.

"Um . . . yes."

"This your first river trip?"

"The first one like this."

"Your job with the B.I.A. in Sacramento, have you been there long?"

"I've just arrived from Washington. The move was sudden, actually."

"That so?"

"Yes. I'm now Acting-in-Charge, Central California Agency."

With all this bingo high-rolling, I thought, maybe somebody had sniffed trouble and gotten out of the way, and maybe Rodriguez would be the designated Poor Fish if anybody raised questions about the bingo operation. According to what I'd heard this morning at breakfast, the outside bingo sharpies had gained the cooperation of three tribal members to pull a fast shuffle, creating something called an Executive Council. The way they set it up, the new Executive Council was empowered to act for the regularly constituted tribal government.

While we were talking, I'd heard a few moving-around noises in the brush behind us. Deer, I thought. But that was odd, they usually lay low during the heat of the day.

Directly behind us, a twig snapped with a loud pop.

TWENTY

AT THE SOUND OF the snapping twig, I'd yelped and jumped to my feet. Behind me, a startled deer bolted and ran, crashing through the underbrush.

Ed looked over at me and grinned, enjoying the incident hugely, while Rodriguez quickly stood and gazed in confusion at the sound of the departing deer. Ed didn't have much opportunity to savor my embarrassment; we shortly saw a trail of dust coming down the road to the opposite bank.

Charlie squinted in the direction of the dusty track, shading his eyes against the noonday sun.

"That's Judy's station wagon," he said, sounding worried.

We gathered at the edge of the stream while Charlie took one of the rafts and paddled across. He and Judy stood by the open door of the station wagon having a conference while I strained to hear their voices over the sound of the water. No luck, of course, but in a moment Charlie got into the raft and came paddling back.

"I'm sorry, folks," he announced, "but you'll have to make the rest of the trip without me."

"I hope nothing's wrong," I said.

"No. Good news, actually. There was a message waiting for Judy at the Palladium office. I'd applied for some grant funding from a San Francisco foundation, and they want me to come in for an interview right away." He grinned. "It looks promising."

Charlie made his apologies to Rodriguez, then took Joe and me aside.

"Ed will take the lead canoe now. You'll each have to paddle single-handed. There's not far to go, but the thrills and spills part is still ahead."

He glanced over to where Ed had engaged Rodriguez in animated conversation. Sissy-pants was listening openmouthed while Ed waved his arms and eagerly pointed down the river.

"Damn!" Charlie said. He called over to Ed and asked him to start loading the lunch gear into the rafts. He turned back to us. "Ed's sense of humor..." He shook his head.

"I'll do the best I can to get Rodriguez bucked up again," I offered.

"You've still got a couple of risky turns coming up—the Mario Andretti and Widowmaker—but the water's high this year, so you should have plenty of cushion going over the rocks. You two

seem to know what you're doing. You know what
to do if you take a spill?''

''Sure,'' I said. ''Feet together, pointed downstream. Let the lifejacket carry you and keep your
arms safe at your sides.''

Charlie nodded, satisfied.

''Does Rodriguez know that?'' I asked.

''Yep. I told him.''

Charlie commandeered Ed to paddle him back
across the river, and Joe and I got busy loading the
other two rafts and fastening everything down
tight, Rodriguez watching us glumly all the while.
When Ed brought his raft back, I kept Sissy-pants
busy in conversation while I made sure his life vest
was on tight.

Then I signaled it was time for us to leave.
''Round 'em up,'' I hollered, imitating Charlie's
style, ''and move 'em out.''

We pushed into the water, Ed and Rodriguez in
the lead boat, me next, and Joe bringing up the
rear. I looked across the river. Judy had apparently brought a change of clothes for Charlie. He
was just emerging from the far side of the station
wagon, wearing a suit and tie, and waving cheer-
fully at us. Charlie looked elegant. Even at this
distance, I judged his wardrobe to be quality
stuff—maybe not new, but the fit was impecca-

ble. The clothes, combined with Charlie's natural physical grace and handsome appearance, made him look ready for even the snootiest of foundation committees.

I'd been steadily revising my estimate of Charlie. First, I'd assumed he was just another college kid who'd taken a summer job as a raft boatman, loved running rivers, and decided to make a career of it. Then, when he was telling us about his first marriage, he'd mentioned his family. They'd had a little money, he'd said. Judging by everything I'd seen, and his ambitious plans for Reliance Enterprises, he'd understated the case considerably. Charlie had that aura of ease and assurance that came from lots of money—old money, most likely.

I'd forgotten to ask Charlie how Judy's interview with the magazine editor had gone. No matter—I could find out later. But that brought up an uneasy thought. Belle had arranged the interview; the message for Charlie had been delivered through her office at *Palladium*. This whole business of separating Charlie from us could be a setup. The most obvious objective would be to get Charlie alone. On the other hand, his unexpected departure left me, along with the rest of us, out here on the river without him. I wished I'd taken time to check the equipment before we left the lunch spot.

We were in midstream now, gliding swiftly toward the next bend of the river. Up ahead, I could hear the unmistakable roar of white water. I turned around and looked at Joe. He held his paddle still, concentrating on watching Ed in the lead boat. I turned back around to do the same.

The stream was deep, and narrowing. My raft picked up speed, splashing steeply around a couple of boulders and then plummeting down toward an especially sharp bend. I could see that Ed had started working his paddle for all he was worth, taking quick, strong strokes to adjust his direction going into the descent. I dug in with my own blade. Scared and exhilarated at the same time, I watched Ed and Rodriguez disappear into the foaming white water. Moments later my own raft slid down the steep, smooth stretch of fast water. Ahead, a huge boulder presided over a sharp turn at the end of the descent.

I made my paddle bite repeatedly into the water. I was trying to do what Ed had done, shift the raft's direction to pull away from a collision course with the big rock. My eyes were glued to the rock and the thin layer of water gliding swiftly over the spot where it jutted into the stream bed. There couldn't have been more than an inch of clearance. My raft slid by, the current carrying me just as it was supposed to and propelling me onward, to shoot down a great V of cascading water and into the pond below. Ed had stopped to wait there, circling his raft in the quiet water. Rodriguez sat immobile beside him, still clutching the edge of the raft. He had a used-up look on his face, and his fancy duds were plastered wetly to his body.

I turned around as Joe came gliding safely into the still water. "Yahoo!" I shouted, waving a paddle. Joe didn't say anything, but he was grinning so big you could *hear* it.

Downstream were a few more gentle rapids, and then one last run through white water. After that the canyon hillsides dropped away from the river, the land flattened, and the water slowed. When the stream carried our three rafts under a highway bridge, I realized we were coming to the end of the trip.

Just beyond the bridge Ed headed toward the left shore. From the looks of things, this was a public beach—a county park, maybe. I could see a group of picnickers at the far end of the beach. Close by was a tree-shaded area with tables and benches and a concrete block set of rest rooms. Judy's station wagon was parked at the nearest end of the parking lot just beyond. She and Rosie were waiting to greet us. Apparently they'd been waiting awhile; Marie had gone down to the water's edge to play and was busily involved in some marvelous game. She was poking a stick in the soft silt and doing little dances around it, too absorbed to notice our arrival. I nosed my raft in to shore, jumped into the shallow water, and grabbed a line to tow my boat up onto the sand. Ed had already beached his raft, with Rodriguez still in it.

Mr. Sissy-pants clambered stiffly out and stood like a post to watch us work. Rosie and Judy came down to help us unload the rafts. As I stacked paddles and life jackets on the beach, I kept an amused eye on Marie. She'd invented quite a little dance. Poke the stick, stomp each foot in the soft silt, hop around a bit, and start all over again.

I was so charmed by Marie's dance that I almost didn't notice when the truck slowed to a stop on the highway bridge, but I heard the faint squeal of brakes, and looked up to see its crimson and gray stripes gleaming in the afternoon sun.

TWENTY-ONE

In an instant, the man in the sweatshirt was out of the truck and poised by the open cab door, raising a rifle to his shoulder. I shouted to warn the others, at the same time dashing toward where Marie danced by the water's edge.

A spout of water rose in the air, inches beyond Marie. Scooping her up, I turned, almost colliding with Rosie and Judy. "Run!" I screamed. "To the rest room." Two more shots came as we stumbled up the sandy, sloping beach.

We were almost on the walkway that led to the concrete block rest room when, still running, I turned to have a look. Joe and Ed, who had been working on the far side of the rafts, were still clambering through the sand. Rodriguez was running in the other direction. On the bridge, the man in the sweatshirt had moved over to the rail and had one foot on it. He braced an elbow on his knee and raised the rifle barrel again.

I heard another shot, and then, almost immediately, one more. I floundered into a bush, almost dropping Marie, but kept moving. Rosie and

Judy had overtaken me now. When we reached the safety of the rest room, I thrust Marie through the door and Judy took her. Joe pushed inside right behind us.

"Where's Ed?" Rosie asked anxiously.

I looked. He was halfway up the beach, sprawled on the sand.

"Ed!" I shouted, but didn't dare go out. I stood in the doorway, with Rosie trying to push past me. I managed to hold her for a minute, despite her fierce struggles.

I heard the truck door slam and let her go as the truck roared away, fishtailing, tires screeching. Rosie dashed to Ed's side, with me close behind her. He was flat on his back in the sand, but wriggling around. Rodriguez and the group of people who'd been picnicking on the beach were running toward us.

"Get to a phone," I shouted at them. "Call for help."

Ed had been shot in the thigh. There was lots of blood; the upper part of his pants was already soaked. I closed my eyes for an instant, almost in panic at the sight. Then I looked at Rosie, tears streaming down her face as she resolutely felt around, trying to see just where the wound was.

"There's a big artery at the top of the leg," I told her. I started pulling off my belt. "We can use this for a tourniquet."

She nodded, and gingerly took hold of Ed's leg. He screamed. She looked at me questioningly.

Ed's leg was oddly crooked—broken. The bullet must have smashed into the bone. We might do more damage moving the leg. But an alarming amount of blood was flowing.

"Got to do it," I muttered.

We fumbled with the belt. Ed kept silent this time. I hoisted his body from the middle, as gently as I could, and Rosie slid the belt under. Then I wrapped it around the top of Ed's leg, put the end of the belt through the buckle, pulled it back tight and hard, and tied the loose end in a knot.

Rosie knelt to cradle Ed's head. I reached down toward his leg, pulled the fabric tight against the bullet wound, and tried to gauge whether the flow of blood was slowing. I wasn't certain. There didn't seem to be much bleeding here, yet a lot of blood was still flowing out into the sand.

"Here. Maybe you can use these."

It was Judy, behind me, carrying Marie in one arm and holding out a wad of paper towels. I took them, trying to decide what to do next. Compression on the wound was supposed to help, but you weren't supposed to mess around with a broken bone.

"I think his leg's bleeding underneath," Rosie said.

The bullet must have come out the other side, making another, larger, wound there.

"I don't think I should do anything else," I said. "I can't risk doing more damage. We might have sharp edges of bone right next to blood vessels."

Rosie turned her face away, and I wished I hadn't let those words out of my mouth.

"The tourniquet seems to be doing it," I said lamely.

Rodriguez came back.

"Those people from down the beach have gone to call for help," he said. "There's a pay phone at the other end of the parking lot."

"Thank heaven the rest of us are okay," Judy said. She was hugging Marie close. I wondered if she realized that those first shots had been fired at her little girl.

"Where's Joe?" Rosie asked.

He hadn't come back with the others. I jumped up and ran toward the rest room. Blood was spattered on the walkway. I hadn't noticed it before.

"Joe!" I hollered.

He was inside, sitting on the floor, propped against the wall. He greeted me with a wry grin. "Don't worry, Emma. He just winged me, I think."

He was clutching a wad of bloody paper towels to his shoulder.

Rodriguez appeared in the doorway. "Is he all right?"

I nodded, moving aside so Rodriguez could come in and see for himself.

"The people who called for help are down there now with Mr. and Mrs. Silva."

"Is Ed hurt?" Joe asked.

"He got shot in the leg," I said. "It's not so good. There's a lot of bleeding." I got down beside Joe, wanting to see for myself whether I ought to worry about him, too. I'd noticed quite a bit of blood smeared on the wall behind him.

"He got me high," Joe said, "just above the collarbone, I think. The bleeding's mostly in back."

I got a handful of paper towels, but Joe shook his head as I approached him. He indicated the wall behind him.

"Had to try it out a few ways." He grinned. "But now I've got my leaky spot pushed square against the wall, and I think I'd best stay put."

I started to protest.

"You go on back," Joe said. "Maybe Ed needs tending."

"Okay."

"Keep an eye on Rosie," he added.

When I got back to the beach, Ed seemed to be only semiconscious. I knelt for another look at the leg. Though it was still oozing a little blood, I thought we'd managed to stop most of the bleeding, even the bleeding underneath.

"What happened to Joe?" Rosie asked.

"He was shot in the shoulder, but—" I'd started to say I didn't think he was hurt as badly as Ed. "I think he'll be okay."

Moments later we heard a siren wailing toward us. Up on the road I could see a truck with flashing lights.

"Division of Forestry fire truck," Rosie said, her voice surprisingly matter-of-fact. "Around here they're usually the closest."

Two firefighters set about tending Ed.

"We've radioed for an ambulance," one of them told me. "The sheriff's department, too."

"The ambulance should be here right away," the other one added. "The sheriff's patrol may take long. They're spread pretty thin in this part of the county."

I stayed for a few minutes, until one of the men said he thought Ed was going to be okay, then I went up to check on Joe. I stayed with him until the ambulance arrived, after which, satisfied Joe and Ed were both taken care of, I headed for the pay phone in the parking lot to call the Fairville police.

I was put right through to Emerson Holmes. As soon as I told him what had happened, he asked me to wait on hold while he had someone put out a bulletin to look for the Damien pickup. Then I spent quite a bit of time on the phone with Holmes, explaining the attempts on Charlie's life. "I don't see what the connection might be to Rebecca's killing, but this is definitely the same man," I told him. I wanted him to say he agreed with me, but, as usual, he listened to everything I had to say, and revealed nothing in return.

By the time I'd finished talking to Holmes, the ambulance had left and a sheriff's car had finally arrived. We gave our statements to the deputies— all of us except Rosie, who had gone in the ambulance along with Ed and Joe.

When the sheriff's car departed, Judy and I were left by ourselves. She'd been able to persuade the deputies to deliver Rodriguez to where he'd left his car in a nearby town. We sat in the front seat of her station wagon, with Marie put down for a nap in the back.

"Maybe you should call Charlie and tell him what's happened," I suggested. "Do you know where to contact him?"

"I have a phone number, but I don't want to call there. What would it look like for the grant application if those people knew about the shooting?"

"I guess you're right."

"I don't want to stay here any longer," she said, glancing up at the road by the bridge.

She started the station wagon and pulled up onto the roadway, turning in the direction of the Madrone *rancheria*. "There's a coffee shop up the road," she said, checking her rearview mirror. "I think it will be safe there. There are usually some people around."

We drove in silence for a time.

"Judy," I said. "The rafts and all the equipment are down there on the beach."

"I know. I was thinking about that. And the Bronco and Ed's truck are still up in the hills."

"We've got a logistics problem," I said. "By the way, how did Charlie get to his appointments?"

"He borrowed Rosie's car."

We considered the possibilities. The first order of business, obviously, was to stop at the coffee shop so that Judy could phone her neighbors and ask for help in collecting the equipment and vehicles.

"I definitely don't want to spend the night at home," Judy said. "That man knows where we live."

"Where else can you stay?" I asked. I wanted to collect my truck from the Moores' barn.

"Marie and I could go stay at Clara's, I suppose."

"What about Charlie? Won't he be coming back this evening? If you don't phone him . . ."

"You're right. I've got to let him know where I'll be."

After some more discussion, we decided to risk a quick trip to Judy's house. She could leave a note for Charlie telling him she would be at Clara's, and I could retrieve my truck. We wouldn't stay there a minute longer than we had to.

I was apprehensive about making even a brief stop at the Moores'. The man in the sweatshirt had obviously thrown caution to the winds, and might do about anything now, including going there and waiting to see if we'd show up.

I was more mystified than ever about his objectives. He could have taken aim at any of us when he opened fire at the beach, but he'd shot first at Marie.

None of it made sense. There was no way to predict what he might do next.

TWENTY-TWO

OUR STOP at the Moore place was a marvel of speed and efficiency. It took us less than five minutes to pack up our things and get my truck out of the barn. The note Judy propped on the kitchen table for Charlie said only that we were at Clara's, and he should come right away.

Judy and I stayed close together as I followed her in my truck back to Fairville. When we pulled up in front of Clara's townhouse, I saw Melissa's car parked in the driveway. Frannie would be there, too, I thought.

It was Frannie who came to the door to greet us. She was bubbling with excitement about something, and didn't seem to notice Judy's overnight bag.

"I was so tickled when Clara said you were coming over," Frannie said. "Gracious! And here's little Marie, too."

Apparently Clara had decided not to tell her mother or Frannie that anything was wrong.

"How was your river trip?" Frannie asked, and then gave us no time to answer. "Oh! I'm so glad you're here in time for supper. Melissa's fixing that wonderful hunter stew she makes.''

Clara had made a wise decision, I thought, saving us from a joint editorial from Frannie and Melissa about this whole affair.

"Come on in to the den," Frannie said. "We're watching the evening news for—oh, I don't suppose you know!" Her eyes sparkled. "Such a scandal! Melissa and I heard it on the car radio when we were going from *Palladium* over to the Plaza West mall. Those bingo operators are in real trouble, and so is that government agency in charge of the Indians.''

Clara came in, adding her explanation.

"This is exactly the kind of help we've needed," she told Judy. "Some reporter from New York broke the story this morning. He arrived yesterday and started asking questions about whether the tribe's executive council was legal.''

It had to be the reporter who was supposed to come on our trip. Charlie must have told him what questions to ask and who to talk to. No wonder Charlie hadn't seemed disappointed that he wasn't coming on the river trip.

Frannie turned up the sound on the television.

"I think the story's on now. Oh, I'm so excited!''

The television newscaster was explaining the way the Madrone tribal council was supposed to operate. Eighteen people constituted the council—that is, all the adult members of the tribe living at the *rancheria*—which should have made the little *rancheria* a rather effective democracy. But three brothers, all members of the tribe, had formed the executive council—apparently with some tutoring from a man described as "a 26-year-old bingo expert from Florida." According to the newscast, the executive council had voted approval early last year for the construction of the bingo establishment.

The news story went on with information about the operation's finances, which had begun to interest me mightily. The bingo parlor, open only four months, had produced enough money to pay off a two-million-dollar mortgage.

"What a lot of money!" Clara said, a wistful tone in her voice. Judy nodded agreement, a grim look on her face.

There were prospects for an audit and an investigation, according to the television reporter. High time, I thought. Maybe this incident would bring things around to where the *rancheria* folks had more say in the bingo operation—and a bigger share of the profit.

"And now," the newscaster said, "we have film taken just moments ago at a news conference hurriedly arranged this afternoon by Bureau of Indian Affairs officials."

There was an establishing shot of Rodriguez, facing a row of microphones, and reading from what seemed to be a prepared statement. Things had really hit the fan about whether B.I.A. should have let this happen, but he had nothing to offer in response except a lot of blather about procedures to be followed before an investigation could be launched.

The reporters must have nailed him right after he'd come back. I marveled that he'd had the chance to change into a suit and tie. This day must have been an all-around bummer for Rodriguez.

"Nuts!" I said.

Clara got up and turned the television off.

"Isn't this exciting?" Frannie said. "You know," she added, looking mischievous, "I made plans this afternoon to go up to that bingo parlor and do a little investigating for myself."

Melissa heaved a martyr's sigh. She rolled her eyes, to indicate she'd tried to talk Frannie out of it.

"Goodness!" Frannie said, glancing at her watch. "I've got to go upstairs and change."

"But dinner is on the table," Melissa protested.

"Oh, you're such an old poop," Frannie said to her. "You know Christian will be here any minute." She started up the stairs. "Don't you remember he said he'd be here in an hour?"

I wasn't altogether happy at first about Frannie's plans, but then decided that maybe an evening at the bingo parlor wasn't such a bad idea. She'd be out of harm's way and maybe with Frannie gone, Melissa wouldn't hang around long after supper. Clara, Judy, and I needed a chance to talk.

"Let's go ahead and eat," Clara said.

"Very well," Melissa said petulantly. "Maybe Frannie will have time for a bite before she leaves."

We began our supper in silence, Melissa making a point of glaring from time to time at Frannie's empty place. I busied myself with Marie, keeping up a lively conversation with her, and hoping the child would say nothing that would reveal this afternoon's incident.

When Frannie came down the stairs, she had on the oddest outfit I've ever seen her wear. She'd changed into a navy blue pleated skirt, with a bright green pullover sweater. The blouse underneath had a Peter Pan collar, and she was wearing penny loafers.

"Isn't this just exactly right?" She spun around to show off her costume. "What do you think?"

"I think you should sit down and have some dinner," Melissa said.

The doorbell rang.

"Oh! That will be Christian."

Frannie scampered to the door. I was expecting to see Whitaker and his eternal smile, but a moment later Frannie came back by herself.

"I'll just grab my purse. Christian wants to leave right away."

Melissa gave her a dark look.

"But your supper!"

"Oh, they serve delicious food at the bingo place. Christian said so. And I'm just dying to have a look around over there."

"Sounds good, Aunt Frannie," Clara said. "Have a nice time."

"Thank you, Clara," Frannie said brightly, avoiding Melissa's gaze. "Well! We'll just be on our way. Bye-bye, now!"

Before Frannie was out the door, Melissa had gotten up, heaved another of her prodigious sighs, and began clearing Frannie's place setting from the table.

"At her age," she grumped, heading for the kitchen, "acting like a silly schoolgirl."

I'd been puzzling over Frannie's outfit, but now the reason for it dawned on me.

"For God's sake," I whispered to Clara and Judy, "she's doing Nancy Drew!"

We were having a good chuckle over that when the door opened and Frannie came back in.

"Something for you, Emma. I almost forgot." She handed me a large envelope. "It came for you this morning just before I left. Express mail, so I thought it might be important."

It was from Neal Stringer. He'd lost no time sending the old issue of the *Globe-Tattler*. I set the envelope aside, trying not to show much interest.

"My, my," Melissa said as soon as Frannie had left again. "Express mail. That *does* look important."

"It's something I sent for," I said.

I was saved from further explanations by Charlie's arrival. Judy jumped up to hug Charlie, clinging so tightly I began to be certain Melissa would notice.

"Good news!" Charlie announced, disentangling himself from Judy and scooping up Marie to give her an enthusiastic hug. "I was hopeful when they called me in for an interview on such short notice, and then . . ."

"What interview?" Melissa asked sharply.

"With the people from this foundation," Judy said hurriedly. "They phoned just this morning wanting him to come in." She turned back to Charlie. "Did we get it?"

"Can you believe it?" he said. "Both the interview and the okay on the money in one day—the entire amount we asked for!"

I was astounded. From what I knew about grants and such, you had to write formal proposals and go through all kinds of rigmarole.

Judy grabbed me. "It's true! It's true!" she shouted. "Ten thousand dollars for Reliance Enterprises!"

Charlie stood there, beaming, while Melissa's expression rapidly shifted from curious to suspicious.

"Who are these people who are giving you all that money?" she asked.

"They're a new outfit, over in San Francisco—the Oracle Foundation."

Oracle. It didn't register for a minute. But when it did, I was flabbergasted. Melissa noted.

"Emma, what's the matter with you?"

"Oracle Foundation," I said, not stopping to think. "I went to see Belle Damien the other day, and saw the word *Oracle* written on her appointment calendar."

Charlie looked stunned.

"Oh," Judy said, "we can't be sure that—"

"That there's a connection?" Charlie broke in fiercely. "You bet we can!" He was astoundingly angry.

"What's all this about?" Melissa asked, looking from one to the other of us.

"Damn!" Charlie exploded in anger. "I've been a fool. She conned us. She wanted us to think the money was coming in because of what we were doing. All those questions about Reliance Enterprises projects, that was all a cover-up. She rigged the whole thing."

I couldn't figure it out. Why would Belle set something up to give money to Reliance Enterprises?

"It's time we went and had a talk with Belle Damien," he announced, pulling on Judy's arm. "Come on. You and I and Marie are going over to her place and have this out with her."

An instant later he'd stormed out the door with Judy and Marie in tow.

TWENTY-THREE

AFTER GIVING CLARA explicit instructions about the proper care and refrigeration of the leftover stew, Melissa left, grumbling about people who weren't civil enough to sit down together for a meal. Her exit scene was magnificent, and I would have enjoyed it hugely under any other circumstances. As it was, I quickly filled Clara in on the details of this afternoon's events, then eagerly opened the express mail envelope.

I had no problem finding what I was looking for. It was on the front page of the *Globe-Tattler*.

A banner headline read "Millionaire Hates Only Son," and, right under it, "Real Estate Tycoon P.J. Damien Announces Disinheritance at Press Conference."

I summoned Clara, who had gone to phone the hospital to see how Ed and Joe were doing. She hurried back and looked over my shoulder at the headline.

"P.J. Damien. Wasn't he—?"

"Right," I said. "Belle's husband."

There was a picture of old P.J. His expression was angry.

"Emma, was he really a millionaire?"

"I don't know, but Belle sure is."

There was a photo inset next to the picture of P.J., a photograph of monumentally bad quality. All I could make out was a young man with a crewcut, unkempt beard, and dark horn-rimmed glasses. The caption said this was the only available photo of Ellsworth Damien, son of P.J. Damien. The picture had been taken a decade earlier in Canada, where he'd gone to avoid military service.

I read the story out loud.

"A fortune made in postwar development of shopping centers and subdivisions by a daring San Francisco Bay Area entrepreneur will be denied to his handsome wastrel son, the father has declared in a dramatic public announcement. 'My son Ellsworth has already distinguished himself in disgrace,' the 62-year-old millionaire announced to assembled reporters and onlookers, 'he shall be given a monthly allowance, but only so long as the estate is being held in trust for my preferred inheritors.' "

The story went on to say that copies of P.J.'s new will had been distributed at the news conference. It also said P.J.'s son Ellsworth had, at 18, rashly married a local waitress, Joanne Traversi, in a "shotgun wedding." That same year, 1946, Ellsworth Damien's new wife gave birth to a daughter. The daughter's name leaped out of the page at me. *Rebecca*.

So Rebecca was a Damien, old P.J.'s grand-daughter.

"Now we know who Rebecca is," Clara said. "Rebecca Damien Higgins."

"Good grief! It's just come to me that Belle was a stepmother. And that would make her Rebecca's grandmother."

"You don't think she was the grandmother Rebecca was talking about?"

"I don't think so. Somehow that doesn't register right with me."

"I wonder if Belle knows about this old story," Clara said. "By the way, how did you know to send for it?"

"Part of this issue of the *Tattler* was left behind in the house where I found the baby. There was also an old *Fairville Reporter*. Both had pages missing. I've already looked up the missing page from the back issue of the *Reporter*. I found an article mentioning P.J.'s press conference, but not really saying what it was about. I figured there had to be something going on that the local newspaper didn't want to print—and the *Tattler* had been all too delighted to use.''

We got back to the article.

''Neglecting his wife and child, and refusing to live with them, Ellsworth Damien moved in the fall of 1946 to nearby Santa Rosa to attend school, enjoying great popularity as a football star on the Redwood Junior College team, but neglecting his academic work. He was, in his father's words, 'a damned wastrel.' The following year, in the classic style of wealthy fathers, P.J. Damien negotiated a bargain with his unworthy daughter-in-law, paying her to agree to divorce and decamp for parts unknown.''

''Rebecca's mother couldn't have decamped for parts very far away,'' I told Clara. ''The two of them lived together before the mother died a while back.''

The article went on with more about Ellsworth Damien. He had been sent, after several years of football and fooling around, to attend a private Canadian university ''through his mother's 'old-money' family connections.''

''That's the first I've heard of Belle's predecessor,'' I told Clara. ''Maybe the first Mrs. Damien decided she didn't have to put up with old P.J.''

"Sounds like she was from an aristocratic family."

"One that had had money. You know, they must have looked down on old P.J. Then he turns around and more or less passes on the snub to his 'unworthy' daughter-in-law."

"I don't think she was unworthy," Clara said. "It said she was a waitress. At least she worked for a living."

Ellsworth Damien apparently had bounced back and forth between Canada and California. The article went on at great length—Ellsworth had wound up marrying a wealthy young Canadian widow, Elizabeth Manning, and fathering another child. But, after "ten years of his frivolity and philandering," Ellsworth's second wife had sued for divorce, and ultimately won the right to keep both her family fortune and her son.

"Good for her!" Clara said.

I'd been skimming ahead in the article. "My God!" I said to Clara. "Look at this. Ellsworth's son by the Canadian wife—his name. It's Charles Manning Damien."

"I don't see—"

"But that's what could connect up the whole thing! Try this on for size. Charles Manning Damien is Charlie Moore."

"Wow. You really think so?"

"You bet. There's your motive. It explains why the man in the sweatshirt wanted to kill both Rebecca and Charlie, and why he took a shot at little Marie. It's Ellsworth Damien, come back to collect the family fortune by killing off all the other heirs."

She nodded. "It could be. Charlie's about the right age."

"And he came from up that way—Canada. If he knew he was related to Belle, that would explain why he was so hot under the collar when he found out she'd sneaked around to give him some money."

"Of course! That's exactly how Charlie *would* react. He'd see it as an unearned handout, charity from a part of the family he'd probably just as soon forget. And not only that, the money was made in real estate development."

According to the article, after Ellsworth's divorce from his second wife, he "returned to his father's home in a reconciliation attempt." He'd also "sought out his daughter Rebecca, who by this time was approaching her eighteenth birthday." Maybe, I thought, he'd tried to cosy up to her and get at the family money that way.

"Young Rebecca, in a move to repudiate both her hardworking mother and her ne'er-do-well father, took up with a young man living a Bohemian life. The rebellious young couple were last known to have been living in a dilapidated mansion on the outskirts of Fairville, a small town east of San Francisco."

"The Queen Anne," I said to Clara.

Rebecca's marriage had apparently been the last straw for old P.J.—he'd gone off on his disinheritance tizzy.

"Small wonder he sent Belle to Europe before he staged the press conference," I said to Clara. "She wouldn't have approved of all this vindictive malarky."

The article said P.J. had not only left Ellsworth out in the cold, but his children, too. "Rebecca, having already demonstrated her foolishness, and Charles, to the best of my knowledge, already exhibiting all indications of being a spoiled brat and likely to follow the wastrel inclinations of his father."

"Old P.J. was in a real snit," I said, having done some quick mental arithmetic. "Charlie couldn't have been more than ten years old at the time. The only thing he was guilty of was being his father's son."

The will, according to the article, provided that the family money should go "to the children, if any, of Rebecca and Charles."

"Maybe Rebecca already had her baby at the time P.J. did all this stuff," Clara said. "Maybe Ellsworth found out about the baby, and . . ."

"And snuffed it," I said. "Sounds likely. But he didn't kill Rebecca then. I wonder if he meant to, but didn't get the chance."

"It's creepy. The whole thing."

"Look," I said. "Here's the rest of the will."

"However, if both Rebecca and Charles are childless upon their fortieth birthday, they may collect the money, upon the supposition that by this time they will either have acquired some sense or be in dire need of cash."

"Rebecca was about forty," I said, "and Charlie is—what do you think—mid- or late thirties?"

"That's about right."

"Then that's why he's come back to do his killing. It was getting down to now-or-never. He'd lose his monthly allowance when the estate was distributed. And it says here, right at the end of the article, that if Rebecca and Charles or any of their children were not living, the money would revert to Ellsworth. Lord! Look how old P.J. put it. '. . . in the unlikely event Ellsworth has not met an unseemly death by then.' "

"Gosh," Clara said. "How awful! Killing his own children."

"I don't know what happened when he killed Rebecca's baby all those years ago," I said, "but I think he planned for everything to look like an accident this time around. He must have thought he could wait awhile after he'd finished the dirty work, and then show up to collect his inheritance, expressing surprise and indignation to be informed of all those inexplicable deaths."

"Maybe he's planning to kill Judy, too."

"I expect so."

"At least now we know who he is and what he's trying to do."

"Yes, indeed," I said, looking again at the grainy, out-of-focus photo of a young Ellsworth hiding behind a beard and horn-rimmed glasses. "And a fat lot of good it does us."

TWENTY-FOUR

I WAS EAGER TO get over to the Fairville police station to show the *Tattler* clipping to Holmes and tell him about Charlie. I phoned, made sure he would be there, and then waited while Clara called the hospital.

"Your friend Joe is doing fine," she reported. "They're going to let him leave tomorrow, but Ed Silva will be there longer. The bullet hit bone and did a lot of damage. They had him in surgery for quite a while."

"What about Rosie? Is she still at the hospital?"

"Yes. She wants to be there with Ed, and she's going to stay overnight."

Clara and I decided that after I got back from the police station, we'd go together to the hospital. We'd agreed I should spend the night with her.

When I arrived at the police station, I was ushered immediately into Holmes's office.

"Thank you for coming in, Mrs. Chizzit. May I see what you've brought?"

His exterior was as impassive as ever, but I suspected he was mighty curious about how I'd managed to get a copy of that back issue of the *Tattler*.

He stood by his desk eagerly reading it. I waited, impatient, studying him. His usual noncommittal expression soon vanished, replaced by sudden pursings of his lips, eyebrows raised in astonishment, and fleeting scowls.

I wondered if Vince had learned anything by following Belle around all day. Maybe he was still over there, parked outside the Damien mansion in his car. If so, he'd witnessed Charlie's arrival, which probably confused him mightily. I'd have to get in touch with Vince—he at least deserved to know I was all right.

Holmes finished reading.

"Mr. Holmes, I—"

He held up his hand.

"One moment please, Mrs. Chizzit."

I waited, annoyed, while he went to the door and summoned the man at the front counter. "Mr. Cooper, please have this document copied."

He sat down at his desk again, pulling out one of his notepads and carefully writing the date and time at the top.

"Forgive me, Mrs. Chizzit," he said. "I know you've been through a difficult experience today, but I have an incomplete picture of this afternoon's event and it will be necessary to ask you—''

I lost my patience entirely.

''Oh, come off it!''

''I beg your pardon?''

''I've had enough of your *procedure*! Why don't you just—''

I stopped myself. I was ready to say plenty, but this was no time and no way to accomplish anything.

''Look,'' I said. ''I've got some things to tell you. And it seems to me that if I knew what you had in mind—if we each knew what the other knew—we'd make a whole lot more progress.''

''Well, yes. . . .'' His face had turned beet red.

''I'm sorry to explode on you like this,'' I put in quickly.

''Actually,'' he conceded. ''Until you brought this clipping in, we didn't have all that much to go on. We were focusing on finding the truck, tracing Rebecca Higgins's background, and so forth.''

''Why don't you focus on what I have to tell you right now. Let's begin with this—I think Charlie Moore is Charles Manning Damien.''

''What makes you think that?''

"Just before I came over here—Judy Moore and I had gone to stay with her friend Clara Edmundson—Charlie came to tell us he'd gotten some grant funding. I recognized the name of the foundation. The money was coming from Belle Damien. When I said so, Charlie blew his cork."

"I don't understand."

"He didn't want to take the money if it was coming from the Damiens. Charity, he called it."

"But I still don't understand why—"

"Why else would Belle want to help the Moores? After all, they were trying to stave off her kind of development at the Madrone *rancheria*. Also, Charlie told us he came from Canada and his family had money. He's about the right age, too."

"Ellsworth Damien's attack this afternoon," he said, "began with shots fired at . . ."

"Right. He fired first at Charlie's little girl. And here's another thing I haven't had a chance to tell you. Ellsworth had already tried to arrange a couple of 'accidents' for Charlie."

There was a knock at the door. The man from the front desk handed the *Tattler* clipping back to Holmes. Holmes sat down at his desk and began scanning through it again.

"By the way," he said. "How did you get this?"

"I checked at the state library in Sacramento and learned that a private collector had it. I called him. He sent me this copy."

He nodded thoughtfully.

"So now we've got the clipping," I said, wanting to get us back on track.

"We certainly do." He glanced up at me. "Thanks to you."

"Now we know who our criminal is. We know his motives, too. We just don't have any suspects."

"Aptly put," Holmes said after a moment. "By the way, this clipping offers a number of opportunities to search for Ellsworth Damien. For instance, we can find out where he has been receiving his mail. According to this article, he's been getting a monthly allowance."

Holmes reached for his notepad. We were back to procedure.

"Belle Damien is probably the executor of her late husband's estate. I'll ask—"

"Where he gets his mail? I don't see how that's going to help us find him here and now."

"Patience, Mrs. Chizzit. That's just the first useful item that we may glean from this clipping. Mr. Damien may also be traceable through his second wife's family in Canada."

"Maybe they'll have a picture. I'd sure like to know who to be on the lookout for."

"Um." Holmes was scanning the clipping again.

"Maybe Belle knows what he looks like—if you can get her to level with you."

He looked up at me inquiringly.

"I went to see her about the initials on the cradle. I think she told me the truth about those, but she was trying to hide something, too. That was the day I saw the word Oracle on her notepad—the name of that fake foundation she set up."

Holmes was scribbling on his notepad.

"First priority," he said. "Seeing what help we can get from Belle Damien."

"In my book, first priority is finding out what Ellsworth looks like when he isn't wearing dark glasses and a sweatshirt pulled down around his face."

I picked up the clipping again and looked at the picture of Ellsworth. Unless he'd grown a beard again and still had a crew cut, it was useless for identification. Then I studied the picture of his father, trying to imagine a younger version of P.J. Damien. The man was as bald as a billiard ball, but otherwise not bad-looking. His forehead was broad, his features large and regular, except for a somewhat hooked nose.

"What do you think Ellsworth Damien would look like now?" Holmes asked. "I mean, if he were clean-shaven, maybe with long hair."

"Who knows? Like his father, maybe."

I tried to imagine how P.J. would have looked if he weren't bald—and without the scowl. What an angry man he'd been, needlessly angry. With all that money, he could have just let his son play around, mess up in school, and....

"Wait a minute! Ellsworth was on the football team when he was going to college in Santa Rosa. We could check yearbook pictures."

"Right." Holmes was making notes again. "I'll have someone go over to Redwood J.C. first thing in the morning and check the yearbooks. Which year?"

I looked through the clipping. "Forty-six. Forty-seven, too, probably."

"Class pictures and football team pictures," he said. "I think we could have those back here for you to look at tomorrow." He leaned back in his chair and looked at me. "I think we've done a pretty good day's work, Mrs. Chizzit. But I'm concerned for your safety."

"I'm not going home. I'll be spending the night here in Fairville with Clara Edmundson."

I got out the number and address and wrote it down for him. I'd just handed it over when the phone buzzed.

"Yes," Holmes said impatiently. "Very well. Put him through."

Holmes listened for a moment, then pushed a button on the phone so I could hear, too. It was Vince, reporting on his surveillance of Belle. He'd followed her to a lawyer's office in San Francisco, and then to the office of a private investigator in Oakland.

"The man's name is Blodgett. I went over and pulled his picture from the concealed weapons permit file. I gotta check with Emma Chizzit to see if it's the guy she saw at that shopping center thing. I been trying to get hold of her. No luck, though."

"Well," Holmes said, "she happens to be—"

I made frantic signals. *Not now*, I mouthed. But I supposed I should talk to Vince sooner or later. I indicated the piece of paper with Clara's address.

"I've been in touch with Mrs. Chizzit. She'll be spending the night here in Fairville with a friend."

Holmes gave him the address and hung up.

"Can you shed some light on what Vince had to say about Belle Damien's activities today?"

"She probably went to see the lawyer in San Francisco about this foundation she's set up to give money to Charlie."

"And the private investigator?"

That had me stumped for a minute, then I realized what Belle might be up to.

"Maybe when Rebecca was killed, she suspected Ellsworth. Of course! She'd known the terms of her husband's will, and it would be just like her to say nothing and try to get a line on him in her own way."

"Perhaps Belle hasn't seen her stepson in years."

"Or maybe never. She was in Europe at the time of the press conference."

Holmes looked somber. "I hope for her sake she has never met him and couldn't possibly know what he looks like."

I hadn't thought about that until now. If Belle knew what Ellsworth looked like, he'd be after her, too. Anyone he thought might know what he looked like was in danger. I asked Holmes if he was planning to talk to Belle tonight.

"The minute you leave," he said.

"Then I'd better be going."

"I suppose so," Holmes said. "And I'm glad you spoke up, about...." He looked embarrassed.

"I'm glad we got around to a little teamwork on this, and I'm sorry for having such a short fuse." I stuck my hand out. "Friends," I said.

"Friends," he repeated, and smiled.

I left feeling rather satisfied, and darn relieved to have some prospect of solving what up until now had been an inexplicable mess. Holmes and I had covered a lot of territory.

"Teamwork," I said out loud as I got into my truck.

Then I remembered something Vince had told me the day he helped me load my doors at the Queen Anne. Vince had played on the Redwood College team. I was certain he'd said 1946.

TWENTY-FIVE

ELLSWORTH AND VINCE had to have been on the same team. I hurried over to Clara's place, hoping Vince would be there.

He'd already come and gone.

"You just missed him," Clara said. "He was here asking for you not five minutes ago. But you told me—well, you know—that he was kind of a pest."

"Did you tell him I'd be here later?"

"No, because when he said he'd go over to Sacramento to see if he could find you at home, I just left it at that. Did I do something wrong?"

I told her what she'd done would have been fine, except that I'd just realized Vince probably knew what Ellsworth looked like. I said I'd tell her more later.

"Maybe I'm off on a wild-goose chase, but I'm going to try to catch him."

I pushed my old Dodge through the Fairville traffic, taking reckless advantage of its size to crowd in front of little hatchbacks and light-weight pickups. By the time I reached the eastbound on-ramp, I'd left behind a trail of honking horns and irate drivers, but I figured I'd probably cut two minutes off the time it had taken Vince. I could catch him if he went straight for my place without taking any side trips, if he held to legal speed on the freeway, and if I'd be able to spot that old Chevy of his—a lot of ifs.

On the freeway I held to a steady ten miles an hour over the speed limit, scanning each car I passed. I finally saw the familiar outline of the big Chevy some distance east of Fairville and pulled alongside, honking for all I was worth. When Vince looked up, registering astonishment, I pointed to indicate that he should turn off. We were almost to the main cutoff north; we took the turnoff and pulled over at the end of the off-ramp.

Vince got out of the old Chevy eagerly, his face wreathed in a huge smile.

"Am I glad I caught you!"

"Jeez, Emma, are you okay? Did everything go all right on your trip?"

"Vince, I've got to have your help. Didn't you say you played football at Redwood J.C.?"

"Right. Hey, I was the star center."

"In 1946? Isn't that what you told me?"

"Yeah."

"Then you were on the team at the same time as Ellsworth Damien."

"Old Ace? Ace Dee? Sure. Gosh, that's right, he was a Damien."

"Can you tell me what he looks like?"

"What's going on? How come?"

"We discovered—I learned a whole lot of stuff today. Ellsworth Damien is the man in the sweat-shirt."

"Him?" Vince asked incredulously. "Ace?"

"Him," I repeated. "Ellsworth is our killer, all right. He's out to get the family fortune. Rebecca was his daughter, we found that out from the *Globe-Tattler*. Ellsworth's father disinherited him—the money was to go to Ellsworth's kids instead. There's more, but the main thing right now is to know what he looks like."

"Ace? Aw, he couldn't—"

"He most certainly *could*. He killed Rebecca. And today, on the river trip, he came sneaking up and took a shot at a little girl. He missed, but he wounded two other people. For God's sake, tell me what he looked like!"

"Well... Okay, he was a real good looker. That's why we called him Ace, he really made out with the women."

"But what did he look like?"

"He wasn't all that big a man, but big enough for a quarterback. He was a great quarterback."

"Try giving me a police description of him."

"He was maybe five-ten, eleven. Can't remember the color of his eyes. Light brown hair, wavy, lots of it. He was real proud of his hair."

"He might be bald now. What else?"

"No scars or tattoos or that sort of stuff. Not much help, huh?"

"Think. What do you know about him?"

"He used to have a motorcycle. Ace was real proud of it. He had this little tool kit—always fiddling to get that bike running just right."

"Handy with tools, that's our man."

"You don't suppose he still has a motorcycle?"

I discounted that idea. But Vince knew what the man looked like. He had to have a clear picture in his mind.

"Vince, if you just saw him walking down the street toward you, how would you know it was Ellsworth?"

"I dunno. But I'd know him. Even older, I *know* I'd know him."

"Close your eyes and try to see him," I said. "Just try to see him the way he might look now."

"Yeah . . . okay. He'd be dressed up. He was always dressed up, paid a lot of attention to how he looked. And he'd have that smile on his face, he was always smiling at women.''

"Go on."

"Well...like I said, he was a sharp dresser. And he did these exercises, you know, to keep his mid-section firm. He probably still does those exercises, that was real important to him. I bet he never let himself get heavy like me—but I'm still real strong, you know that.''

"Sure," I said. I was getting an idea I didn't like.

"Well, I guess what would really cinch it would be the outline of his head. Like I said, he had this big head of hair. Come to think of it, he had kind of a large head, too. Yessir, you always noticed Ace—all that hair, his looks sorta made me think of a lion.''

"Leonine."

"What?"

"No wonder he knew exactly where I lived!''

"Who?"

"Christian Whitaker—that's what he's been calling himself. He's the guy who's been dating my friend Frannie.''

"Oh-oh."

"And she's with him tonight.''

"You think he might ... ?''

"He came and turned on the gas in my place, didn't he?"

I was thinking a mile a minute. Frannie was in danger, all right.

"Ellsworth Damien can't afford to have anyone around here recognize him, not if he thinks he's going to come back later and claim the inheritance," I told Vince. "He must have used the Christian Whitaker identity to do some snooping, and then maybe he saw a chance to pick up a little money on the side from Frannie. A rich widow from out of town, she'd seem like a safe enough opportunity."

"Yeah. But she turns out to be Belle's friend. Oh, my gosh!"

"They went up to that bingo place on the Madrone *rancheria*."

"We could go up there. I got a set of cuffs in the car. I could—come on, get in my car."

"There'll be a lot of people up there, and Ellsworth's probably got that revolver he used on Rebecca. We can't—"

"We can't wait around, Emma. I got a radio in the car, so I can call for backup while we're on the way." Vince waved impatiently toward his car. "Come on. Where is this place, somewhere up the Madrone valley?"

"I'll take the truck and you follow," I told him.

"Okay, whatever but we gotta get going."

"It's north from here," I said. "When we get to Woodland, turn off on Highway 16. If we get separated, I'll wait for you there."

"Don't worry. You're gonna think I'm glued to your bumper."

I took the overcrossing to head north. Checking in the rearview mirror, I could see that Vince was already talking on his radio.

As I drove, I tried to anticipate what we would do. Holmes would use up a few minutes rounding up some men and getting a car on the way, and they'd be coming from the other side of Fairville. They'd have to be twenty minutes behind us, maybe more. We'd have time to go in and spot Frannie and Ellsworth, but we'd have to have a plan. We'd have to know what to do if Ellsworth started to leave with her.

I had to assume Ellsworth had taken Frannie to the bingo hall in the first place. That would make sense. He might be desperate by now, but he wasn't stupid. He wouldn't take the risk of trying to pull anything early in the evening. It hadn't been dark yet when he left with Frannie. Whatever he was going to do would be far easier in the dark—safer for him. Come to think of it, he was definitely still trying to play it safe. When he'd come for Frannie at Melissa's, he'd stayed outside. He wanted to keep his hit list down to a manageable size.

Once they'd started back, he'd probably turn off the main road and drive to an isolated spot somewhere. Frannie wouldn't notice—when somebody else was driving she never paid attention. But I was sure they'd still be at the bingo hall. Ellsworth wouldn't risk trying to get her away from there before the evening's events were over.

I tried to imagine what they'd be doing in the bingo hall. He'd be watchful, tense, biding his time. Frannie, in full Nancy Drew mode, would likely be having a wonderful evening. In her bright green sweater and penny loafers, she'd be eagerly snooping her way around the bingo emporium, smiling a sweet little smile all the while and acting super mysterious. Damn! That could set him off.

TWENTY-SIX

BY THE TIME we arrived at the bingo establishment, I'd decided Vince and I should go on and try to get Frannie out of Ellsworth's clutches. I mulled over possible excuses why Frannie had to leave with us—each seeming more inane than the last—as Vince and I circled through the parking lot. We finally found two spaces in the very last row at the far end.

I explained my plan.

"Just get her out, huh?"

"Right. I'll think of some kind of malarky."

"And we should have backup pretty quick. Our guys are on the way."

We walked toward the entrance.

"Jeez. This is some place."

"Yep."

Vince paused outside the big glassed-in entry hall for a quick survey.

"They got a lot of security here, but private guys. Bunch of cream puffs, I bet."

"Let's play it close to the vest, Vince," I said. "I don't want to attract any more attention than we have to."

He pulled the door open for me, and I stepped quickly ahead of him and looked around. Beyond the lobby area was a huge room, with row after row of tables. There must have been a thousand people in there.

"Welcome to Trapper Creek!" a cheery voice called.

A woman, seated at a big table to one side, was beckoning to me. "Sign in here, please." she said, speaking rapidly. "First pack, twenty dollars. Additional packs, ten dollars each. And getaway pack, ten dollars."

"What?"

"You really should get the getaway pack, too. You have a better chance. Book of eleven, six on."

"Uh..." I looked over the huge room.

"This your first time?" the woman asked crisply. "If so, you get half price on the first pack."

People were lining up behind us. Vince went for his wallet.

"Look," I said to the woman. "We're just here to get my friend."

"You have to buy a pack to go in. Sorry."

Vince flopped open his wallet. "Vince Valenti, Fairville police," he said, official as all get-out.

People were looking at us. This wasn't the most unobtrusive way to get in.

"We have to get my friend," I said. "Because, uh... there's been an accident."

"That's right," Vince put in. "An accident. Bad accident."

She looked uncertain and leaned forward to get a better look at Vince's ID.

"Oh, then our security people—"

"Don't bother," Vince said, using a tone of voice that said he was in charge of the world. "We'll find her."

He took me by the elbow and steered us through the entrance and around the corner. He kept us moving, past a cluster of bingo attendants in black pants and white shirts and down an aisle of bingo players. The players were all intent on what they were doing, listening to a voice that came from loudspeakers at every other row. Except for the steady drone of numbers announced by a disembodied voice, the place was eerily quiet.

There was barely enough space to walk between the rows. None of the attendants acted as if they saw us—they were all too busy watching to see if any of the bingo players needed help. The players, seemingly mesmerized, steadily marked their bingo sheets with fat marking pens that printed round spots. Some were playing several cards at once, blotting out the numbers with incredible speed. Plumes of smoke from cigarettes went up toward the high ceiling in rows of wavering lines.

"Smoking section," I said to Vince. "She wouldn't be here."

We squeezed past the players and attendants to the back wall, where a line of people waited at the food counter. I could smell fried chicken.

"Keep going," Vince said. I bumped against a woman with six bingo cards in front of her.

"Can't you look where you're going?"

"Sorry."

Vince urged me on. We were now opposite the entrance. I could see the bright-voiced woman at her desk in the lobby, surrounded by people waiting to get in. Four security guards stood nearby, staring blandly at nothing.

"Okay, let's take the near half of the rows first," Vince said. "I'll look for Ellsworth and you look for Frannie."

I saw her almost immediately.

"There she is!" I whispered to Vince.

They were concentrating on Frannie's bingo cards, their heads almost touching.

"See? Green sweater and—"

"Jeez! It *is* him!" Vince pulled back a little ways, as if he expected Ellsworth to look up and recognize him.

A moment later Ellsworth got up and leaned over to say something to Frannie, then started down the aisle. We did a quick fade—backing up against the wall—and Ellsworth made his way to the end of the aisle without seeming to see us. He turned quickly in the other direction and walked toward the food counter.

"Now's our chance," I said.

We pushed out way down the aisle to where Frannie still concentrated on her bingo card. I hunkered down and whispered her name. She looked up, blinking with surprise.

"Emma! What on earth are you doing here?"

I glanced over toward the fried chicken line. Ellsworth stood immobile, staring straight ahead with a look of patient fortitude.

"Frannie, there's no time to explain. You've got to come."

"But—"

I reached over and took her purse. "It's an emergency." I stood up and tucked the purse under my arm.

"Goodness gracious!" She half-reached for her purse. "You look so grim! Did something happen to you?"

"We've got to leave. I'll explain outside," I said. I backed away from her toward the other end of the aisle. She followed, making a tentative try at retrieving her purse. I chanced a look back to see if Ellsworth had noticed us. Incredibly, he was still in line, facing the other way.

"Come on, Frannie."

I moved her as fast as I could, Vince backstepping behind me. We reached the end of the aisle, and I stepped aside to move Frannie ahead of me. She collided with Vince.

"This is Vince Valenti, Fairville police," I told her.

"Oh, my!" She stuck out her hand automatically. "Pleased to meet you."

"You have to come with us right away," he said. Then, taking advantage of the fact that he still had hold of Frannie's hand, he pulled her along. He put his other big paw on her shoulder, propelling her efficiently toward the lobby.

"But, I can't just—what about Christian? He's getting our dinner."

"We'll notify your friend later," Vince said, again sounding as official as all get-out.

"Frannie, we've got to go. Look, Vince can use his police radio—call back and have him paged for a message."

We made it through the lobby, moving swiftly, and hustled Frannie straight out the front door. No one paid any attention to us. The minute we were outside Frannie planted her feet and balked.

"I won't move another inch! You've got to tell me what this is about."

"We've discovered the identity of the man who killed Rebecca," Vince said.

"He shot at little Marie, too," I added. "We've got to leave here right now."

"Gracious! Was Marie hurt?"

"No, but—"

"Please, ma'am, let's keep moving. I've got a vehicle out in the lot."

Frannie looked dubious, then capitulated.

"For goodness' sake, Emma. You could at least give me my purse."

I surrendered it, at the same time taking a quick look back into the lobby. "Everything's okay," I told Vince. "We're in the clear."

He was looking toward the highway.

"No backup yet," he said. "That's funny. They were going to call the local sheriff's patrol."

"We can't count on seeing a sheriff's car right away," I said. "At any rate, they were awfully slow this afternoon."

Frannie shot me a questioning look.

"After the shooting," I said. "A fire truck and the ambulance got there first."

As we hurried Frannie through the parking lot, I kept glancing back toward the brightly lit entry. This had been too easy.

We reached Vince's car and he opened the door on the passenger side for Frannie. I could see that his old Chevy was indeed a decommissioned police car. There was a radio on the dash, a spotlight, just about every piece of equipment except one of those holsters for mounting a shotgun vertically amidships on the dash.

Vince closed the door quickly behind Frannie and trotted around to take his place behind the wheel.

"I'll be following," I told him.

Instead of getting in my truck, I stood watching as Vince's receding taillights jounced around the corner at the end of the row and toward the parking lot entrance. I waited until I saw him turn onto the highway and then, satisfied, turned back toward the bingo hall. I planned to make certain we had gotten away as cleanly as we'd seemed to. I just wanted to make a quick check from the entrance. Nothing would make me feel so comfortable as the sight of Ellsworth wandering around inside with a couple of plates of fried chicken in his hands and a confused look on his face.

TWENTY-SEVEN

I HADN'T HEARD Ellsworth coming up behind me. He caught my left arm in a viselike grip, and, at the same time, pressed the barrel of his revolver against my right temple.

"Don't make a sound."

His fingers dug into my arm as he pulled me backward into the darkness and then propelled me in the direction of my truck. I moved forward, unresisting, momentarily numb with surprise. We were almost to my truck before I spoke, surprising myself at how nearly I was able to keep to a conversational tone.

"You saw us."

"I'm not blind."

I took a cue from the contempt in his voice. "I guess we were pretty dumb."

"Exquisitely stupid, as a matter of fact."

He brought us to an abrupt stop by my truck. "Now, if you will be so kind...." He gestured, assuming an elaborate gallantry, and indicated I was to get in.

"I thought it was odd you never turned around. In fact, I hadn't left yet because I wanted to see—"

"Move!"

He shoved. I opened the truck door slowly, stalling for time. We'd been inside the bingo hall maybe ten minutes, with a few more to get Frannie to Vince's car. It would be another five minutes, probably more, before the Fairville police showed up.

"Get in, dammit!"

But Vince would encounter the patrol car coming up the road and flag them down. They'd stop to wait for me. I started to climb into the truck, then tried another conversational tack.

"I thought you might be curious about why we came to get Frannie ... Mr. Damien."

He jerked me backward and spun me around.

"Don't play smart with me!"

He was using one hand to keep my arms under tight control behind my back. The revolver in his other hand was only inches from my nose.

"You thought you were so frigging smart in there." He brought the barrel up, aiming it directly between my eyes. "You thought I didn't see. The hell I didn't!"

He put the barrel of the revolver right up to one of my eyes. "I saw," he said with a vehement bitterness. He took aim into my other eye. "I saw it all."

I tried to keep from blinking. He found that amusing. He laughed, holding the gun in a more relaxed way, aimed rather generally at my chest.

"The whole charade was priceless. The two of you talking your stupid cow of a friend into leaving."

He released his hold on my arms, stepped back, and again gestured toward the open door of the truck.

"If you please, madame."

Moving deliberately, I put my left arm forward, as if to steady myself climbing into the cab, then reached ahead with my right hand. My ax handle was still on the front seat, right where I'd left it the day I'd been so nervous about going inside to check the old Queen Anne.

"Wait."

He glared at me suspiciously, then waved me back with the revolver.

"Hold it. Stay right there."

Keeping the revolver trained on me, he reached back with one hand to feel around on the truck seat. A moment later he chuckled and pulled out the ax handle.

"You've been trouble right from the start," he said, examining it thoughtfully. "Maybe I ought to use this on you right here and now."

I tensed, considering my chances for success if I made a run for it. Then he threw away my ax handle. It made a high arc over the front of my truck and disappeared in the bushes beyond.

"There's no point in killing anyone else now," I said. "You'll never be able to claim that money."

"No?"

"The police know who you are."

"The police—that clown you brought with you tonight? My dear woman," he said and shook his head in mock sadness, "don't underestimate me. There is an enormous difference between what the police think they know, and what can be proved in a court of law." He smiled maliciously. "Who can identify me? One policeman, Frannie, possibly Belle Damien." He shrugged. "A manageable list."

Manageable. On top of killing Charlie and his family.

"And then, of course, there's you." He waggled the gun no-no style in front of my face. "You should have been smart enough to stay out of this.

But you couldn't leave it alone, could you? You had to come snooping around. That money is rightfully mine. I'm supposed to have it. I should have had it all along, was going to have it, until my father..." his voice had been growing louder, and curled venomously around the word *father*. "... my idiot of a father changed his will."

I stayed quiet, not daring to say a word. I'd gotten him talking.

"God! Do you know what he did to me? Do you have any idea how I've had to live?"

He put on one of his Christian Whitaker smiles. " 'Time for some bubbly, my dear.' " He held the smile at full wattage, crooking an arm as if offering to escort someone. " 'Ah, my lovely lady, where shall we go this evening?' " The smile vanished. "All those years ... all those incredibly stupid women."

He seemed completely self-absorbed, studying the gun in his hand for a long time, although he still had it aimed squarely at me.

"And now nothing is going according to plan ... nothing. Do you realize what an absolute bitch of a time this has been for me?"

I looked back at him as steadily as I could, nodding to indicate sympathy.

"Shit! You're stalling." He motioned impatiently with the revolver. "Get in the truck."

I climbed in behind the wheel. He was right behind me, keeping the revolver just inches from my head.

"Slide over."

I slid over.

"The keys—hand over the keys."

I got the keys out of my pocket and held them out to him. He climbed into the truck, switched the revolver to his left hand, took the keys, and put them in the ignition.

"Now, lovely lady," he said, "we'll just go for a little ride."

He reached out to pull the truck door shut with his left hand, which still held the revolver. It was now or never. I slammed my elbow into his ribs with all my might and followed through, swinging both feet up and shoving him out of the truck.

He hit the ground hard, but as I struggled across the seat toward the open door I was astounded to see him roll as smoothly as if he were a gymnast. Just as he came to his feet, a flare of car headlights swung past.

Inexplicably, I saw Frannie, less than ten feet behind him. There was no mistaking that crazy sweater and skirt outfit. Her eyes were wide with fright, her hands over her mouth. She seemed to be screaming, but I could hear only Ellsworth.

He was yelling obscenities, an unending stream of them. I'd assumed from the smooth way he'd rolled to his feet that he'd kept his wits about him, that he'd kill me swiftly and efficiently. Mouthing those vile words, he moved with surprising deliberateness. As he approached, I saw his progress in a series of flashes from car headlights—his face was livid with rage, coming closer and closer, strobe-lit, eyes bulging, nostrils flared. Tears, glittering in the stop-motion glare, coursed down his cheeks and into the smile creases at the sides of his mouth. The revolver trembled as he brought it up to take aim. I was frozen, seeing nothing but the wobble of the gun, the open mouth of the barrel—then, in the glare of circling headlights, Vince's hunched form rushed forward. Head and shoulders down, he charged, bellowing as he slammed into his old teammate.

I recovered my wits and hurried to jump down from the truck and retrieve the gun. There was no need, really. It was all over.

TWENTY-EIGHT

THE FOLLOWING SATURDAY—only three days later, though it seemed like much more—Frannie and I were on our way to visit Ed Silva in his hospital room.

Frannie scanned room numbers, at the same time juggling her purse, a bottle of champagne, and another of sparkling cider. She also had a clutch of helium-filled balloons. I carried a bundle of plastic cups and a huge tray of her best homemade hors d'oeuvres. Frannie's party-giving instinct had come to the fore, the excuse this time being Ed's release from the hospital scheduled for the next day.

"Here it is!"

Frannie pushed the door open with one hip, allowing me to go in first. Ed, in bed with his cast-encrusted leg elevated, signaled hello with a wave. Vince jumped to his feet from his seat beside the bed.

"Emma, am I glad to see you!"

He charged forward, ready to give me a bear

hug. I escaped by handing him the hors d'oeuvres tray.

Frannie, busy finding places to arrange all the party fixings we'd brought, quickly commandeered Vince to move things around. I settled down for a talk with Ed, at the same time feeling a little guilty about avoiding Vince. After all, he'd saved my life.

I thought again of how Vince had looked when Ellsworth was being led off in handcuffs. He was disheveled and dusty, with great circles of sweat under his arms, his uniform shirt untucked, and his head framed by a sparse halo of hair in the glare of the patrol car headlights. Holmes was there by then, of course, with a contingent of Fairville police. When Holmes had come striding briskly forward, Vince had sprung to attention. Suddenly aware of his appearance, he'd tried to tuck in his shirt and slick back his hair at the same time.

That was Vince! Stalwart, brave, true, kind, sweet, eager... and I didn't want him wrapped around my neck.

"Emma," Frannie said, "please go down to the nurse's station and see if you can get some ice to keep these drinks cold."

I complied. By the time I got back, Rosie had arrived, bringing Joe. He greeted me with a grin as Clara and the Moores trooped in. Belle and Holmes also showed up a moment later.

Frannie and Rosie had been busy with the plastic champagne glasses, setting the tops onto the stems.

"There, the last one," Frannie announced. "Our timing's just right." She bustled around the room, filling glasses. When she was done she proclaimed a toast to Ed's recovery.

"I'll drink to that," Ed said, raising his glass higher than any of us.

"The doctor says he'll be just fine," Rosie added.

"And," Frannie said, still holding up her glass, "a toast in honor of our very own hero—Vince Valenti!"

Vince about to down his champagne, hesitated, obviously uncertain of the etiquette of drinking a toast to himself.

"Drink up, Vince," Charlie said. "Three cheers!" He jumped to his feet and led us in some vigorous hip-hip-hoorays. Vince blushed from his too-tight collar to the roots of his thinning hair.

"Three cheers for the man who saved Emma's life," Charlie reiterated.

"Aw, Emma was doing okay. I just came along and finished the job."

Vince eagerly launched again into his explanation of how he'd realized I hadn't followed him out of the bingo lot, and how he'd come back, only to discover that Ellsworth had me at gunpoint.

"You shoulda seen it, him holding the gun on Emma, and her cool as a cucumber. I couldn't do nothing, even if by then my backup was there. He had that gun on her all the time, right to her head. We couldn't do nothing."

He looked to Holmes for corroboration. Holmes nodded.

"Yessir. Then he made her get in the truck. I was awful scared what he'd do. But, right away, she kicks him back out. He lands on the ground, just like that." He paused, looking around at his audience. "Ker-blooey, out on the ground!"

"That's right," Frannie said. "I saw the whole thing."

"Yessir!" Vince beamed at me. "Ker-blooey!"

"Don't forget," I said, "you were the one who stopped him. He still had the revolver."

"Aw, yeah. Well, it's like I been saying, Emma. Even a lady like you needs someone to take care of her sometimes."

Frannie stood, her glass raised high.

"A toast to three wonderful people," she said. "Ed, Vince, and Emma."

We downed our glasses. Ed and Joe returned to their attack on the tray of food Frannie had brought. They'd made short work of the asparagus tips and dip, and were starting in on the cheese puffs.

"Mr. Damien," Holmes said to Charlie, "I haven't had a chance yet to ask. Were you aware of the terms of your grandfather's will?"

"No," Charlie said. "I scarcely thought of myself as a Damien. I grew up in Vancouver with my mother, and she'd taken back her maiden name, Dodsworth. She didn't want to have anything to do with my father and his family, not after she realized he'd married her for the Dodsworth fortune."

I was watching Belle, who looked plenty interested.

"There was a messy lawsuit after mother's divorce," Charlie went on. "He wanted more money." He shrugged. "I guess I wound up with the idea I'd make a go of it entirely on my own— no asking anybody for money." He looked at Belle. "I want to apologize again," he told her, "for being so angry with you."

"Did you know all along," I asked Belle, "that Charlie was a Damien?"

"Yes, she did," Charlie said. "All these years, she's been keeping track of me." He went over to Belle and took her hand. "By golly, I've got me a grandmother!" He winked at her. "Pretty good-looking, too," he said, turning to the rest of us. "Just think—she's Marie's great-grandmother."

"Gracious! She certainly is." Frannie beamed with pride.

"She's smart, too," Vince added. "After that baby turned up, she put two and two together and figured maybe Ellsworth was involved. That's why she hired the P.I., the guy Emma saw her talking to at the shopping center."

"Actually," Belle said, "I should have gone to the police instead." She looked apologetically at Holmes. "But I wasn't certain the baby was Rebecca's child, or that Ellsworth was the murderer. Of course, I found out years ago about that press conference, and I knew Ellsworth had come around afterward, terribly angry. I suppose he took Rebecca's baby and . . . did what he did. I'm not sure. He must have more or less gone berserk. At least, he made himself unwelcome at every bar in Fairville. Apparently P.J. arranged through a lawyer to have him paid to leave town."

"What about the cradle?" I asked. "You told me there was no one in the Damien family with the initials *AD*."

"The *D* doesn't stand for Damien," Charlie said. "It stands for Dodsworth. Amelia Dodsworth was my mother's mother—actually Amelia Dodsworth Manning. I'm certain she must have given the cradle to Rebecca."

"Oh, my!" Frannie said. "I'm so glad Rebecca had something nice like that to treasure." She sighed. "Rebecca seemed to have so little."

"That brings up the question," Holmes said, "of ownership of the cradle."

"Under the terms of my contract with Emma," Belle said, "it belongs to her."

"If it's mine," I said quickly, "then I want Charlie and Judy to have it. With a baby on the way, I'm sure they can put it to good use."

"Goodness!" Frannie jumped up and gave Judy a hug. "Congratulations."

Joe seemed as pleased as Frannie, though he made a great deal less commotion about it. "If you'll let me have that cradle for a bit, after I get my arm out of this sling," he said, "I reckon I can get it slicked up some."

Frannie thought that was a wonderful idea. "When it's ready, we'll have a celebration—a cradle party. You're all invited."

I looked around the room, thinking what a miscellaneous group we'd make. Charlie and his family, Joe, Rosie and Ed, and Clara. Holmes, too. Clara and Holmes would undoubtedly become a project for Frannie the Matchmaker and Vince.

My gaze connected with Vince's. Old Lonely squirmed, ducking his head and grinning sheepishly at having been caught watching me. I'd immediately looked the other way—and just as immediately felt ashamed of myself for not wanting him to be at the party.

A few minutes later we were milling around, getting ready to go home. Vince positioned himself by the door, ready and waiting as Frannie and I started to leave.

"Emma, you still got to finish your job at that house. Maybe I could come over and give you a hand."

I was ready to make some excuse, but Frannie was too quick for me.

"What a lovely idea, Vince," she said. "It just so happens that Emma told me she'd be working there tomorrow. I'm sure the two of you will have a delightful day."

I grabbed Frannie's arm and propelled her out the door and down the corridor.

"Frannie!" I hissed.

"Oh, come on, Emma," she said, digging an elbow into my ribs and smiling her best mischievous smile. "A lady, even one like you, needs a man to take care of her sometimes."

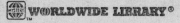

Author of *Mom Doth Murder Sleep* and
Mom Meets Her Maker

MOM AMONG THE LIARS
JAMES YAFFE

STRANGE BEDFELLOWS

Everybody talks under the influence of Mom's chicken potpie—
especially her son, Dave, an investigator with the public
defender's office in Mesa Grande, Colorado. Discussing
cases with Mom has become routine—her logic and rattrap
brain have helped him solve many murders.

Amid the heat of a tight political race, Edna Pulaski, a local
madam, is murdered. The prime suspect is a homeless derelict.
The case seems open-and-shut, and the district attorney, who is
up for reelection, wants a fast conviction. But Mom's got a nose
for exactly the kind of hanky-panky going on in Mesa Grande's
corridors of power. So does the killer.

"A lively and entertaining mystery…" —*Publishers Weekly*

Available in April at your favorite retail stores.

LIARS

BLOODY TEN
WILLIAM LOVE

First Time In Paperback

PRODIGAL SON

So the unofficial partnership of a cynical New York private eye and a cantankerous Catholic bishop was strange—especially since this nice Jewish gumshoe moonlighted as a clerk for the archdiocese. But it paid the bills. And when one of Davey Goldman's cases got too tough, he pulled in the heavy muscle: the bishop loved putting his brainpower—all 220 IQ points—on the matter.

When Jim Kearney's long-lost brother, Nick, comes looking for trouble, he asks Davey to mediate. But before Davey can earn his money, Nick is dead—and Davey has committed the slightly illegal act of shielding the number-one suspect...his client. He's not above dodging the cops or falling in love with his client's girlfriend, either. Just don't tell the bishop.

"A well-developed cast, tightly structured plot and cleverly placed details end with the bishop's questions in an 11th-hour, nail-biting conclusion."

—*Publishers Weekly*

Available in March at your favorite retail stores.